'Work always comes first with you, doesn't it?' she said on impulse.

'I see,' he said, with a touch of complaint in his voice. 'You think that while I was making love to you I was in the operating theatre in my mind? For heaven's sake, Veronica, what sort of callous beast do you think I am? Was I that mechanical about it? Maybe I was too over the top to notice, but I could have sworn you were up in the clouds with me.'

'Oliver,' she implored, 'you know I was completely out of this world, you were wonderful! I didn't mean that.'

'Then what the hell were you implying? That I can be that good and still have time to consider the hospital, or does my work have to compete with you—ah! I understand, I think. Like all women it has to be all or nothing—total commitment to you?'

'You're a doctor, I know the score,' she said. 'I can't hope to compete.'

Helen Upshall lives in Bournemouth with her husband, now retired. When quite young she became interested in Doctor Nurse stories, reading her much older sister's magazine serials instead of getting on with the dusting, so it was a natural progression to go into nursing in the late 1940s. Since she took up writing, ideas have come from a variety of sources—personal experiences of relatives and friends, and documentaries on television.

New England Nurse is Helen Upshall's tenth Doctor Nurse Romance. Recent titles include *Doctor from the Past*, *Sister Stephanie's Ward* and *Candles for the Surgeon*.

NEW ENGLAND NURSE

BY

HELEN UPSHALL

MILLS & BOON LIMITED
ETON HOUSE 18–24 PARADISE ROAD
RICHMOND SURREY TW9 1SR

*First published in Great Britain 1988
by Mills & Boon Limited*

© Helen Upshall 1988

*Australian copyright 1988
Philippine copyright 1988*

ISBN 0 263 76018 9

Set in 10 on 10 pt Linotron Times
03–0388–62,350

*Photoset by Rowland Phototypesetting Limited
Bury St Edmunds, Suffolk
Made and printed in Great Britain by
William Collins Sons & Co Limited, Glasgow*

Dedicated to the memory of my dear
New England friend and colleague,
Natalie E. Carlson, who introduced
me to the lovely State of Connecticut
and gave me Brookville, the location
and staff of which is entirely
imaginary. My thanks to her family
and friends, especially the late
Cora Harris with whom we stayed,
also my aunt and cousins in Rochester
who contributed to making our
Vacation '81 so memorable.

CHAPTER ONE

A TELEPHONE bell clanging much too close to her ear woke Veronica Summers, and she wondered how American mechanism differed from British to create such a rasping tone. With an unsteady hand she picked up the receiver and said a sleepy 'Hello' into the mouthpiece in order to cut off the offending sound.

'Six forty-five, Miss Summers,' a female voice echoed tonelessly. 'Your early call.'

Veronica mumbled her thanks and turned over to give herself time to get a hold on herself—then she remembered that today the much-talked-about Dr Linley was going to be back from his holiday. She sat up on the side of the single bed and rubbed the sleep from her eyes. She must endeavour to be at her best, but after her night out with the girls she wasn't too sure that she'd be able to concentrate, especially as the girls had seen fit to being rather obvious to their male colleagues at Brookville Hospital as to their whereabouts for the evening.

Veronica, after several years of nursing, had learnt the art of waking up smartly when a situation required that she did, so without further ado she went along to the bathroom and took her usual morning shower. In less than an hour she was on her way down the two flights of stairs, out into the early morning sunshine and en route to the hospital, which was only a short drive away. She parked the car in her allotted space and went inside the staff entrance where she clocked in before making her way through long busy corridors to the Accident and Emergency department, and then into the Outpatients area. Thanks to Natalie Craven, head nurse at Brookville, Chrissy, the receptionist for Dr Linley's clinic, and Dave Wilfroy, his registrar, Veronica had found her new job at Brookville interesting and had settled down to her strange surroundings quite quickly.

7

Dave had been particularly helpful and Veronica liked him a lot, but today, she had been warned, there was likely to be less familiarity in the department. Dr Oliver Linley, a thirty-six-year-old bachelor, was, like herself, English, and by repute a stickler for some of the good old-fashioned British ethics of medicine, not always appreciated by some of his American colleagues.

'You should get along just fine,' Natalie had told Veronica on her arrival a month ago. 'He'll be tickled pink at having a girl from back home on his team, which is why I've scheduled you to start in Outpatients. We'll move you around if we can during the year you're with us.'

Veronica had looked forward to meeting Oliver Linley until rumours had reached her of his being some-what temperamental, but then, she reflected, now that she had got to know some of her nursing colleagues she knew they were capable of teasing her, so she must wait and find out for herself just what the great man was like. It wasn't altogether reassuring, though, when a few minutes later a tall, suave figure came striding briskly across the waiting area, back as straight as a ramrod, head erect and eyes looking neither to the left nor right as he endeavoured to avoid direct eye-to-eye contact with any of his waiting patients. She'd need to make allowances today, she supposed, as the first day back after a holiday was always difficult. With a sigh she braced herself and went into his consulting room, where she found him putting on his white coat as he idled over a folder of notes spread out on his desk.

'Mrs Peters ready, Nurse?'

'I think——'

'We don't have time to think, Nurse, you should know that,' he snapped. The unfamiliarity hung like a stiffened curtain between them and Veronica went cold all over as she recognised the man who had helped her on Kennedy Airport the day after she had arrived in America a month ago. Her confidence suddenly evapo-rated just as it had done on that never-to-be-forgotten day.

'Well? What are we waiting for?' He swung round to
face her and then just stared. 'Goodness me! What have
we here? The damsel in distress. You were coming, I was
going, but you didn't tell me your destination was
Brookville. Someone should have informed me that we
were expecting a nurse from England, perhaps we could
have timed things better, at least arranged for me to
accompany you here on my return. Kennedy's not the
most welcoming of airports—but you found your way
here all right in the end.' He suddenly smiled down at
her from his six feet one inch height, his vivid blue eyes
twinkling with what she could only describe as a 'telling'
smile. 'Tell me,' he urged, 'what did you think of our
Pilgrim Airline? Cute, isn't it?'

'I had been warned by a fellow passenger,' Veronica
explained, 'but such a small aircraft was a bit scarey after
a big jumbo.'

Oliver Linley sat back on his hands resting on the desk
as he surveyed her curiously. 'Glad now that you didn't
turn around and head for home?'

'Oh yes,' she agreed readily. 'It was all worth it, I'm
loving it here.'

'Good. Afraid you chose a bad night to travel. You
started off with a delay from Heathrow, then fog here
in New York—still, you were given accommodation in a hotel, though when we met at the United
terminal I can't imagine why that desk clerk was
being so unfriendly—maybe she'd had a bad night or
something.'

'I don't mind being accused when *I* have done something wrong, but it really wasn't my fault that I wasn't on
the computer,' said Veronica. 'The clerk at Kennedy
altered my ticket when I couldn't travel on to Groton
that night as planned, so he should have seen to it. After
all the hassle I really did feel like turning round and
going home!'

'Then it was a good job I happened to be at the same
desk as you, and knew Jim, the pilot. Everything was all
right when you got to this end, I take it?'

'I rang Brookville as instructed and they sent a car for

me. I didn't expect to meet you again, let alone here, but thanks again for your help.'

He inclined his head and the 'telling' smile was back, making her feel awkward.

'They shouldn't let unseasoned single girls loose on their own in my opinion—maybe you haven't done much travelling?' he queried.

'I've never experienced any trouble before,' Veronica said haughtily, her hackles rising in her own defence. She hadn't travelled abroad that much, and certainly not solo. There had been holidays with her group of friends which included various boyfriends over the past few years, but then when her mother had been taken ill she had given up her post as Sister of a women's surgical ward in a busy London hospital and gone home to nurse her. Friendships had been few and far between after that. She was hardly ever free, and no sooner had her mother died than her father had a heart attack. No, for the past two years life seemed to have been held in limbo as it were, but now at last she was free of any domestic ties.

'Travelling in America is a little different from the UK,' Oliver Linley said.

'I've been abroad on holiday, Italy, Holland and Tunisia.'

'But not alone?'

'Well—no, not exactly,' she admitted.

'You're here on this exchange scheme, I take it?'

'That's right, for one year.'

'I daresay arrangements can be made for you to stay longer if you find it hard to leave us at the end of a year,' he told her.

'That isn't likely, as my father lives alone. My sister is looking after him at present,' said Veronica.

Her thoughts flew back to home and she wondered how Ellie was coping. Her sister was younger by eight years and at seventeen was slightly scatty. She'd done the hippy bit, and had recently gone punk, but to please their father she had agreed to stay at home and study while running the household so that Veronica could carry out their mother's dying wish. It had taken them all by surprise when Rosalie Summers had expressed a wish that an attempt be made to trace her father in America. They knew that she had been the illegitimate child of Betty Smith and an American soldier who had gone back to the war in France not knowing that a child was on the way. No one had ever suspected that it had become an obsession of hers as she grew older to trace her father. Before she died she revealed to Veronica that her mother had been secretive about the affair, insisting that the American GI, Burt Duvall, couldn't be traced, but after Betty Smith's death, letters had been found which had aroused Rosalie's curiosity. Veronica's father considered that the whole thing should be allowed to die a natural death, but Veronica's interest was stirred enough to promise her mother that she would do all in her power to trace the family if she could, though she had little enough to go on. Not too much money either, so that only when this opportunity arose to exchange nursing posts with an American girl did she even consider trying to keep her promise.

'We'll have to see if we can't change your mind for you, Veronica,' said Dr Linley. 'Now, let's go and see Mrs Peters, I don't like patients being kept waiting any longer than necessary.' He led the way into the first examination room. 'Hullo there, Mrs Peters,' he greeted cheerfully. 'I have some reassuring news for you. According to the radiologist there's only a shadow there, but I'd like to examine you again to satisfy myself that nothing has changed since I saw you last.'

Mrs Peters was forty-two, a pretty woman with ash-blonde hair, who had recently had a mammogram test which had shown up a suspicious shadow. The patient's eyes were wide and glassy, giving a graphic portrayal of her fear as she sat sideways on the couch, her nicely shaped bosom exposed. Oliver squeezed and probed gently, his solemn expression indicating his intense concentration. 'If there was a mass there I'd be able to feel it, and I can't, so there's nothing to worry about,' he said softly. 'Come and see me again in six months' time, before if you're bothered, and we'll do another mammogram.' He turned aside to write on Mrs Peters' notes, and Veronica helped the woman down from the couch.

'That must be a relief, Mrs Peters,' she said.

'You're English!' The woman sparked into life, and Veronica smiled and nodded. 'How I love that accent, and how I'd love to go to England some day.'

'Spoil yourself, Mrs Peters,' Oliver Linley intervened. 'Take a holiday as a thanksgiving present to yourself, I know just how worried you must have been, but you could have seen Dr Wilfroy in my absence, you know.'

'I guess I was quite happy to put off hearing the result, Dr Linley, and anyway, someone would have sent for me if the news had been really bad. I'd rather hear it from you.'

'Now that you have you can start living again. Which part of England did you particularly want to visit?'

'London, I guess, but there's no chance with two kids to see through college.' She laughed and gestured her hopelessness with her outstretched hands, but she was smiling with obvious affection for Oliver Linley, and Veronica wondered if he had this effect on all his patients. He nodded his goodbye and departed into the next examination room, while Veronica helped Mrs Peters to dress.

'I'm really pleased that there's no cause for concern,' Veronica said encouragingly. 'Sometimes these shadows show up for no reason. You can examine yourself for small lumps, but I expect you've been shown how to do it?'

'Thanks, Nurse, yes, I was referred here by my own doctor and he's going to set me straight, but I am grateful to you and Dr Linley for your reassurance. It's a load off my mind, I can tell you—and one day I will make that trip to London!'

Veronica experienced a modicum of satisfaction. It was so rewarding to see a patient's mind eased in this way. She could name a dozen such cases who, in the past, had gone home with confidence restored from her

ward in London. It was as if the period before her two
years away from hospital life had caught up with her. She
was immensely content to be back doing the job she
loved, and frequently forgot the real reason she had
come to the States. That reason posed some difficulty
—not only did she have too little information about her
grandfather's family, but they had lived in Rochester, at
the northern end of New York State, and here she was in
Groton, Connecticut, a small but very beautiful New
England state on the east coast. She had drafted out a
letter to the Army headquarters to enquire after Burt
Duvall but had so far declined from sending it. She felt
inadequate for the task, realising how vast the States
were and how hopeless her quest, but her mother,
Rosalie, wouldn't have made such a request without
careful thought.

'Veronica!' Oliver Linley's voice sounded urgent, so
Veronica followed Mrs Peters out of the cubicle and
hurried into the next one where he was waiting by the
couch on which lay an elderly lady who was clutching her
bag tightly.

Veronica had expected some reproach for being
longer than he anticipated, but instead he was smiling in
his charming way.

'Here you are, Mrs Walcott, a surprise for you—a real
live English nurse!'

The old lady screwed up her eyes and peered at
Veronica. 'That so?' she said slowly with a hint of
disbelief. 'And what might she be doing in Connecticut?'

'On an exchange scheme,' he told her.

'Actually I've come to try to trace my grandfather's
family,' Veronica explained, 'but I've very little to go
on, so I don't hold out much hope, but it was my
mother's wish before she died that I should try to find out
more about her father.'

'A bit like looking for a needle in a haystack,' Oliver
Linley said cryptically. 'But I wish you success. Now,
Mrs Walcott, you won't cause Veronica any trouble, will
you?'

'As if I would!—well, I'll be blowed, a nice young

Brit, like I was when I first came here as a young bride.'

'Mrs Walcott is a special client of Brookville, Veronica, though she doesn't altogether trust us,' said the doctor. 'She's over ninety and about to undergo surgery for the first time. It's only a small operation, and we want to do a few tests and give her a few days' holiday at the same time.'

'Don't try to soft-soap me, young man! Ninety-three I may be, but I'm nobody's fool. Once you've got me in here I'm not likely to go back to my own home again.'

'How do you like that, Veronica? We're doing our best for one of our own countrywomen and she talks like that!' He lifted the patient's wrist and felt her pulse, shaking his head in mock disappointment as he did so. 'You're good for a long while yet, Mrs Walcott, and we're going to see that you do go back to your own home, fit and well.' He looked at Veronica and smiled. 'A minor digestive problem, that's all, so we're going to see if we can make things a little more comfortable for her.' He turned again to Mrs Walcott and bent low to speak to her. 'We've got all the X-ray pictures, so we're going to take you along to a nice room overlooking the grounds and you'll be first in OR tomorrow. No sneaking cookies and chocolate to bed with you either, but in a week's time I promise you I'll bring you a box of chocolates myself.'

'I'll keep you to that, Dr Linley,' Mrs Walcott said in her shaky high-pitched voice.

Veronica recognised the remnants of a Midlands or North Country accent, and after Oliver Linley had left she asked: 'Which part of England did you emigrate from, Mrs Walcott?'

'Birkenhead. My husband got a job on the railroad here and worked there until he retired. He had a chest complaint and died at seventy-two. Little did I think I'd still be here twenty years later. I've had a good life though, grateful for good health mostly, and at least being able to look after myself. Time's running out for me now, though, and I don't want to be a burden to my friends and neighbours.'

'Have you any family?'

'No, never had any children, I'm sorry to say.'

'And you never went back to Birkenhead?'

'Somehow never got around to it when my Ralph was alive, and then it was too late. Wouldn't be anyone around now who I'd know.'

'Do you live far from here, Mrs Walcott?' Veronica asked her.

'Just a drive along route ninety-five, near Groton airport. Nice little house, used to be a government one until we were able to buy it. My own little garden which I've always loved, and good neighbours—what more could I ask?'

'I'm sure you're going to be fine again when they've made you more comfortable. It's marvellous what the medical profession can do these days.'

'Ah—I'm not complaining, though sometimes I feel a bit nostalgic for England. Wouldn't have minded taking a trip, just to see my old home town once more before I die.'

'I doubt that you'd recognise it, everywhere changes over the years,' Veronica told her.

Mrs Walcott nodded in agreement and a young man came in with a wheelchair to take her along to her room. Outside, as Veronica accompanied her, they met Oliver Linley again. 'You can look forward to a nice long rest now, my dear,' he said compassionately.

'Eternal one, you mean,' grunted Mrs Walcott with a wicked twinkle up at him.

'No, I don't mean that—now you just listen to me —don't you dare let me down.' He placed a hand against Mrs Walcott's cheek. 'I'll let you borrow Veronica here to take special care of you, how would you like that?'

'Sounds kind o'nice.'

'I'm going to keep her for this morning, though,' he said, smiling down at his patient, then adding in a whisper: 'Just to check her out for myself and make sure that she's good enough for our youngest New Englander!'

He guided Veronica along to his office. 'She's got

plenty of spirit left and in spite of her being a bit tetchy at times is a dear. I hope you don't mind being assigned to her, but I know it'll please the old lady.'

Veronica ventured to ask a few questions about Mrs Walcott's condition and discovered that an offending piece of gut needed removing. 'I shall do the least that's possible, but as you must realise, Veronica, at ninety-three the odds are against her surviving for very much longer. I must remember to see Natalie and tell her I've found the ideal place for you to work for the next few days. I want to get Mrs Walcott on her feet and back home as soon as possible. She'll recuperate better in her own home.'

'She has someone to look after her?' Veronica asked.

Oliver Linley smiled thoughtfully. 'She's lived alone for the past twenty years, but she has good neighbours and a host of friends.'

'Isn't there a danger of sending her out too soon?'

He looked surprised that she had dared to question him, then he shrugged and said: 'When you reach the age of ninety-three where would you rather be?'

Veronica raised her eyebrows. He had made a point, and having made the old lady a promise to see that she did return home he intended to keep it.

'Shall we get on, we're running late,' he commented shortly. He was the efficient surgeon again, and the morning continued, with the waiting room becoming overcrowded and a brisk exchange of patients between his consulting room and the two examination cubicles.

Veronica later reflected over a much needed cup of coffee with Natalie that she had learned quite a bit about Oliver Linley in the few short hours she had spent working with him. He certainly had charm, and at times was quick to frolic when occasion called for lighter moments. Mostly, though, he was serious, informative and above all, kind. It was evident that his patients depended on him, that they believed in his judgment, and so far Veronica couldn't fault that judgment even though she had been searching for some flaw however small. He has to be wrong sometimes, she thought, no one could be that perfect.

From the window in the cafeteria Veronica could see the shining water of Groton Reservoir. The River Thames, which had to be crossed to go into New London, flowed busily along to the west. Everything reminded her of home, especially the sea, which was never more than five miles away in any direction, with Long Island Sound in the south. The lush green lawns around Brookville's buildings where peacocks strutted with a stately pride peculiar to them, trees and shrubs helped to span the three thousand miles between this New England and her home. She tried not to think too much about it and refused to acknowledge her twinge of homesickness, but she couldn't help but wonder how Ellie would manage. Her father was not an easy man to cope with. His heart condition had stabilised, which was why Veronica had decided that she could risk going off to leave him in Ellie's care. But Ellie was the favourite, so no doubt would please him whatever she did. Veronica could see her now, tall, nicely rounded and good-looking like their father, with jet black hair and clear, large eyes, a replica of him in his youth. Her own reflection crystallised in the plate-glass window opposite where she sat, and it was as if her mother had materialised to reassure her, to remind her of the task she had given her. Only the colour of their eyes differed between the sisters and their parents. Ellie's were sky blue like her mother's, while Veronica's were soft grey-green like her father's, but she had red brown hair with a porcelain complexion and features identical to her mother. That was why it had to be she who had to try to find her grandfather and his family. There could never be any doubt about her ancestry, for elder daughter, mother and grandmother were like peas from the same pod. Veronica sighed—but what an impossible task!

'Mm . . .' said Natalie, 'that sounds like the sigh that says why did I come to America leaving family and friends, etc., etc.'

Veronica blinked away the vision of her mother and

smiled wistfully at the senior nurse. 'I can't escape from the reason I'm here, Natalie, and it isn't only to gain experience of nursing, which is important to me. My grandmother was a kind of war bride, I suppose, only never a bride. My mother was the illegitimate daughter of an American soldier and she requested before she died that I should come over to try to find my grandfather and/or his family. My sister Ellie is the one who likes adventure, but probably because I have the likeness to my mother and grandmother she specifically asked me to try to trace our American ancestors.'

'But that's terribly exciting!' Natalie exclaimed. 'Did your grandfather come from New England?'

'No, Rochester, the far end of New York State, which isn't a great deal of help, is it?'

'No problem, Veronica. You'd have to go back into New York and it's an hour's flight from there to Rochester. Couple of hours and you can be there. You're in touch with them, I take it?'

Veronica laughed outright. 'No, it's absolutely crazy. I have nothing to go on at all. It seems my grandfather remained silent after the war, he's probably dead by now and I shall be an embarrassment to the family, *if* I ever find them. I've written to the Army Headquarters but not posted the letter yet—I mean, is it really sensible to rake up the past for unsuspecting people?'

Natalie considered this thoughtfully. 'There's always a danger in digging skeletons out of cupboards, but Americans are fairly broadminded and most love to think they have a connection with the UK. I'd say go ahead and see if you can find them, it would be quite an achievement.'

'It's time, though,' Veronica explained. 'My first commitment is to Brookville. Unfortunately I couldn't afford to just come over on an extended holiday to search.'

'But there must be people and places you can write to? Start now, Veronica, the weeks soon fly past and once you've established some connection then you can have a long weekend off to visit them.'

'You sound more enthusiastic than me—and I must get enthusiastic about returning to duty. By the way, Dr Linley has suggested that I follow old Mrs Walcott through while she's in. Is that OK?'

'If Oliver says so who am I to argue? That's if it suits you?'

'I don't mind, anything, anywhere—it's all experience, and variety is the spice of life, so they say.' With a laugh Veronica stood up and left the head nurse to return to the afternoon clinic.

The waiting room had filled up again and she noticed a woman with a small child happily playing pat-a-cake in the corner, and by the window an expressionless, painfully thin young woman who should have worn a wrapper marked 'fragile.'

A patient was just leaving Oliver Linley's consulting room. Evidently he didn't stop for food or drink, so Veronica went to take over from the nurse who had covered for her. Dr Linley was replacing the telephone as she entered. 'You stay with Mrs Walcott for as long as she's in,' he ordered. 'Seven o'clock tomorrow morning, in OR by seven-thirty. Now, we'll have the baby next.'

'Shouldn't you have a break? There's still a crowd out there,' Veronica suggested.

'That's what I'm here for. I told you I don't like keeping people waiting any longer than is necessary.'

'But surely you'd work better after a break?'

'Are you suggesting that I'm not up to standard? *Your* standard, that is?'

Veronica flushed dark red and wished she had kept her thoughts to herself. 'I was only trying to be helpful,' she said.

'And I appreciate your concern, my dear. I wouldn't enjoy eating and drinking knowing that some of my patients were getting exasperated at the long wait, worrying about what they might be about to hear and anticipating a long journey home whether by car, bus or train. I like to work through, Veronica, but I also like my nurses to be fresh and alert, so a break for them is important—besides, there's adequate staff here. Yes, I know, Dave could cover for me, but after a month away I have some catching up to do and patients expect to see me. Now—Larry next, please?'

While the mother undressed the baby in one examination room Veronica took the delicate-looking girl into the adjoining one. She noticed from details in the folder that she was suffering from a blood disorder and she knew that this made the patient listless and exceedingly tired. 'Dr Linley won't be long now,' she assured the young woman, and went to tell Oliver Linley that his patients were ready for examination.

'Young Larry had a strangulated hernia—any observations, Veronica?'

'Looks robust and healthy enough to me.'

'Good, and Jenny Pearson?'

'Cause for concern, I'd say. I've peeped at her notes, but I felt as soon as I saw her that a "handle with care" ticket would be appropriate.'

'Good girl—we'll do just that, handle her with care, have her in for a rest possibly and monitor her blood. Her mother died from cancer, so she's anticipating the worst. She's worried herself into this state, so it's our job to convince her that she isn't suffering from an incurable disease. She refuses to believe her own GP, so he referred her to me about three months ago. She isn't responding, and I need to know why, although, as I say, I feel sure it's a case of worry. I'll need to take time for a chat, so we'll see young Larry first.'

He indicated that Veronica should go ahead of him, which she did. She was very much aware of this man's vibrant energy, which struck out of him forcefully like lightning. She had been aware of his self-confidence the day they had met at Kennedy Aiport, aware and grateful too for his willingness to get involved with a stranger suffering some difficulty in communication. She'd hardly had time then to notice his handsome features, features which she now saw were etched with lines of experience, and in spite of his 'telling' smile there was deep compassion in his expression. His blue eyes could be humorous, intense, or sympathetic. At over six feet he felt like a giant beside her, but there was something comforting about his protective strength, and it was only when he bent to speak to Larry Baker that Veronica noticed that his dark hair was slightly greying at his temples. At first sight she would have said he was in his early thirties, but now she put his age at between thirty-six to thirty-eight.

'Hullo, young Larry,' he greeted the gurgling baby, 'and how's your mother today?'

Mrs Baker, nearing forty, Veronica thought, smiled vacantly up at him as she exposed her baby's abdomen. 'Grateful that this is all over, doctor,' she said wearily.

He felt the tiny incision which, though pinkish in colour, was healing well. 'He's doing fine, which is more than you'll be if you don't get yourself sterilised, Mrs Baker. Nine children are enough for the healthiest of women, three or four too many for you.'

'I'd have had twelve if I hadn't had those three miscarriages,' Mrs Baker said, tossing her head defiantly. 'I'd have loved them all, doctor,' she added with an emotional crack in her voice.

'I know you would, my dear, but we are expected to respect our frail bodies, Mrs Baker. Your children, thank God, are all a sight healthier than you. Just tell that fifteen-stone husband of yours you need a holiday.'

'He's a good man,' Mrs Baker pleaded.

'Tell him I said you need a check-up soon. Blood tests, blood pressure—bet you haven't been back to your GP for yourself since Larry was born?'

The woman shrugged as she looked at Oliver Linley with a certain coyness. He chucked the baby under his chin, patted Mrs Baker on the back hopefully and went out into the corridor. 'I'll never understand women,' he said impatiently. 'She's anaemic, she's got swollen ankles, and a diabetic too. What can you do with a woman who worships her lustful husband and refuses to tackle the inevitable result?'

'Not a lot,' Veronica answered with raised eyebrows.

He grinned suddenly. 'You're right,' he said. 'Why

should I worry? Maybe she enjoys bed romping as much as he does.'

Veronica tried to pretend that her cheeks hadn't coloured with embarrassment. She was well used to doctors making flippant remarks from time to time. They were human, after all, and being forced to deal with so much tragedy needed a safety valve. She doubted that she would be capable of coping with a couple of children, let alone nine, and she knew that Mrs Baker's weary pallor meant that she was far from well, as the doctor had stated, but they both knew that she was the type to be submissive to her husband, and in a strange way they admired her courage.

'The trouble is,' Oliver Linley said, 'I do worry. If she wears herself out who will care for nine children? I must write to her GP and get him to have a tactful word with Mr Baker—it won't do much good, I suppose, but it's the least I can do.'

They went into the next cubicle where Jenny Pearson lay on the couch expecting the worst.

'Hullo, Jenny,' Dr Linley said cheerfully. 'We'll soon have some colour in your cheeks now that I've got some results to go on. How are you feeling today?'

'Getting more and more tired. Don't patronise me, Dr Linley, I know my fate and I don't really want any treatment. Chemo-therapy is so distressing, it was for my mother, so I'm opting to let nature take its course.'

'Splendid!'

Jenny Pearson sat up straight and stared at him in disbelief. 'You can't help me?' she accused.

'On the contrary, Jenny dear. We can help you, but best of all you can help yourself. Do you want me to be honest?'

'Can I take it?'

'Of course. You haven't been eating or sleeping, so you've brought about your own downfall. Yes, your blood is very tired, Jenny, but only from lack of nourishment. I gave you pills—where did you put those? Flushed them down the john, I suppose?'

For the first time Jenny's cheeks showed some colour

as she turned bright pink. 'I didn't think it was worth taking any medication,' she said falteringly. 'I honestly couldn't take all the treatment my mother had. It was painful, and sometimes very distressing, and it didn't really help her, did it?'

'It didn't cure her, no,' Oliver Linley agreed, 'but it prolonged her life and made her feel that she was worth caring for, now surely that was right?'

'I'm not convinced that it was,' Jenny argued stubbornly. 'But I understand you've got your job to do. Please don't raise false hopes in my case. I know I'm getting weaker.'

'You're absolutely right, and if you refuse help then there's no point in your wasting any more of my time.'

'You're angry with me.' Her huge eyes filled with tears and she looked from the doctor to Veronica for help.

'Yes, Jenny, very angry. You're an attractive young woman with your life before you, and it's our job to do everything in our power to save life, but we do need your co-operation. What I have in mind is not very drastic, but it's entirely up to you. I'd like you to come in for two weeks while we give you a blood transfusion and monitor your progress. With the correct diet and rest for that time you should walk out of here a new woman.'

Jenny stared at him defiantly, disbelief in her expression, then she was forced to turn away from him.

'Think of it as a holiday if you like,' he suggested. 'Go home to think about it, but don't take too long. Alternatively I can arrange for you to see someone else to discuss it with, if you'd prefer that?'

'A psychiatrist, you mean? No way! I'm not off my head, Dr Linley,' she said with contempt.

'I wasn't suggesting that you are, my dear, but perhaps another woman doctor, or even Veronica here, to talk things over with. You know the old saying, a trouble shared is a trouble halved, and that I believe is true. It's not my job to pressure you, so I'll see the rest of my patients now and hope that you'll get in touch with me very soon.' He closed the folder of notes, pushed them into Veronica's hand and turned to leave.

'Wait!' Jenny called after him, and suddenly a deluge of tears flowed freely. 'I . . . I'm sorry.' Oliver Linley waited patiently while she sobbed, sniffed and blew her nose. 'I . . . I'll come in as you suggested.'

'When?' he asked curtly.

'Whenever you like—I haven't been able to go to work for the past three weeks.'

'Veronica, take Jenny to the coffee lounge and get her a drink while I see Natalie about a bed,' he ordered.

Veronica was surprised at his brusqueness. Had he lost patience, or was it his ploy to make Jenny comply with his wishes? By the hard, distinct tread as he walked away she somehow felt that he was quite capable of losing his temper with anyone who didn't see things his way, and at that moment Veronica's sympathies were with Jenny Pearson.

She helped the patient off the couch and guided her outside, along the corridor to a pleasant room overlooking the garden where only one or two people were waiting to be collected.

Jenny sighed. 'Am I really being stupid? I wonder if he knows what it's like to watch your own mother, who was my best friend too, waste away, and all you can do is to stand by helplessly.'

'I've only recently met Dr Linley,' Veronica explained, 'but his reputation is one of compassion, and I'm sure he's only doing what he thinks is right for you. A gynaecological problem could be causing some anaemia, so it's sensible to come in and let Dr Linley thoroughly investigate the cause.'

'You make it sound so easy,' Jenny said. There was almost condemnation in her voice.

'It's easy for us to delve into a problem with the patient here and willing to do all that we ask. It's not easy for you—I know that,' Veronica consoled. 'How long since you lost your mother?'

'Three years, and you're going to tell me I ought to be getting over it by now.'

'My mother died less than two years ago, so I can appreciate how you feel. Sometimes I ask myself will I ever get over it. We're only human, we question the fairness of it all, but I couldn't bear to see her suffer —and yet she was so kind and uncomplaining. She worried far more about me having to nurse her, give up having a good time, than about her own condition and the fact that she would never get better. She never wasted a moment of the days when she was well enough to keep occupied. She wrote letters, did some beautiful embroidery, watched television and took an interest in all kinds of projects. The people who really have cause for moans and groans seldom grumble about their situation.'

Jenny smiled at Veronica, a warm hopeful smile, and Veronica felt heartened. 'I'll try to think more positively,' she promised. 'Mother didn't complain either, but I felt so much of her pain for her. I loved her so much, we only had each other, my father went off years ago, so we lived for each other. I felt nothing but hatred and bitterness after she'd gone, and I believed when I began to feel ill that I was being punished.'

'You've been punishing yourself, Jenny. Perhaps blaming yourself for living when your mother was taken. It's natural, but don't blame yourself. Your mother wouldn't want you to, would she? Make a good life for yourself and do things you know she'd be pleased about. What kind of work do you do?'

'I'm a computer programmer, and I really enjoy my work—or did until I began to feel so wretched.'

'Not married, or engaged?'

Jenny shook her head sadly. Veronica guessed there was more personal sadness than the fact of her mother's death, but she didn't want to appear too inquisitive. Jenny sat back and waited while Veronica went to fetch a tray of tea and biscuits, then she stirred in her sugar thoughtfully.

'From High School on I always had admirers, so I guess I found it pretty hard when I was restricted to staying at home to look after Mum. After she'd gone people were very kind, one man I worked with was a little too attentive and I suppose I fell for him because I was in a vulnerable state. Too late I discovered he was married. He didn't want to break it up. Selfish brute, he wanted to have his cake and eat it too, but at least I proved myself strong where he was concerned. I told him where to go and I still stuck it out at work, in spite of the gossips talking about us. Then six months ago I heard of a job in New Haven, applied for it and got it, so I've been there ever since, but I'll likely lose it if I don't soon get well. I've been in the throes of whether or not to move down there to live, but as soon as someone comes to look at our house I know I want to stay where memories of Mum are the strongest.'

'Maybe you're trying to move too quickly,' said Veronica. 'It takes some folk longer than others to adapt. Get well first, then you'll get a clearer picture of where you want to be. It was easier for me in that I had my father and sister Ellie. Now there's a crazy, mixed-up kid if ever there was one!' Veronica laughed, and by the time she had related a few of Ellie's pranks to Jenny, the younger girl's eyes were sparkling with amusement.

Jenny was on her second cup of tea when Veronica was paged to take the patient to the ward.

'That's good, they must have found you a bed,' Veronica said cheerfully, but one look at Jenny told her that all her old fear had returned. 'I'll keep popping in to see how you're doing. I'm to special an old lady of over ninety who came from back home when she was a young bride. She's a real tonic in herself, so when she begins to recover from her operation maybe you'd like to visit her?'

Jenny grabbed Veronica's arm. 'Nurse, I'm terrified,' she confessed. 'I can't . . .'

'You can and you will,' Veronica said firmly. 'Everyone here is lovely. It's like a big happy family, and you're lucky to be under Dr Linley.'

'I know, so everyone tells me. He isn't married and he's the darling of Brookville.'

'Then see that you're his number one success.'

When they reached the small room Natalie was waiting and she seemed to be showing some impatience.

'I'm sorry,' Veronica apologised in a whisper. 'Dr Linley told me to take Jenny along to the lounge to have a cup of tea. She's very nervous.'

'It's OK, Veronica, I'm not mad at you. Sometimes Oliver gets up my nose! He had no business to put you on the wards. Oh, super for Mrs Walcott, but you can't be spared just to special her all the time. I've just had a fight with Sir, but of course he always wins in the end. I appreciate you had to do a stint on the wards eventually, we want you to have a session in most departments, but you're particularly good in Outpatients. I expect you've found it a change from a busy surgical ward, haven't you?'

'Yes, a pleasant one, but I really don't mind where I work. I certainly don't want to be the cause of any friction between you and Dr Linley.'

Natalie laughed. 'Oh, that's nothing unusual. We enjoy a love-hate relationship. I just object to his interfering in my domain, that's all.' She turned to Jenny. 'I'll be along later to take all your particulars, Miss Pearson. Right now I'll leave you with Veronica and she can help you to settle in. See you later, Veronica.'

Jenny took stock of her surroundings and Veronica knew that she was remembering when she had visited her mother in this same hospital. Later on they discovered that Mrs Walcott was just along the corridor, so Veronica took Jenny in to meet her, before going to the day-room where there were other young women of a similar age to Jenny.

By the time Veronica was able to return to the Outpatients Department the waiting room was empty and there was just the clearing up to finish. Veronica went into Oliver Linley's consulting room, surprised to find him still sitting at his desk.

He glanced up as she entered and raised his dark well-groomed eyebrows.

'I'm in the doghouse, in case you haven't seen Natalie,' he said.

'I have—and I'm sorry.'

'What for? You didn't ask to be moved. I'm rather

impulsive, Veronica, and if I get a sudden brainwave it gets put into practice before anyone can argue. Natalie does argue, frequently.' He seemed to be amused at his own private thoughts, and Veronica wondered if there was anything between him and Natalie. Then he sat back in his chair and faced her casually. 'In this instance I was considering my elderly patient, and Jenny as well. You can hover between the two—only don't tell Natalie I said so.'

'Dr Linley!' Veronica protested. 'You're making me piggy-in-the-middle.'

'It's quite nice to have a girl from back home. The English are excellent peacemakers.' He waved a hand over the work on the desk. 'When you've finished here we'll go to the canteen together. I'm interested in hearing all about your plans for finding your grandfather, but—hum—well, Veronica, have you really thought of the anguish you might be about to cause?' he shrugged. 'To a family, perhaps?'

Veronica stared at him with a vacant expression for several seconds. 'I'm only doing what my mother wanted me to do,' she excused herself, but in that moment she understood why she had not been able to send off the letter to the Army Headquarters.

CHAPTER TWO

IT WAS AN hour later that Veronica clocked off duty and she would have gone to the canteen alone. Oliver Linley had been called away, but now, as she left the nurses' station, she collided with him.

'Ah, trying to sneak off without me,' he joked. 'Of course I don't want to keep you if you have a date or anything, but I thought it might be nice to catch up on things since we met a month ago.'

'I—I intended to go home and have my meal there,' she lied, her brain rushing on ahead warning her that she actually had nothing in the fridge suitable for a main meal and she was hungry.

'I'm sure whatever you've prepared can keep,' he insisted, and he promptly turned around and accompanied her to the lift. Veronica stood in one corner and decided that this was a big mistake. He had questioned the reason for her being here, which made her feel uneasy even if she herself had questioned the wisdom of carrying out her mother's wish. She wanted to go ahead with her plans to please her mother, but she had used the plan in order to gain her freedom, if only for a year. Ellie was the favourite, the one everyone had to consider, the apple of her father's eye, so it was only right that she should now be taking over the role of housekeeper for a while. Hadn't she, Veronica, done her bit?

She sensed Oliver Linley gazing at her. His eyes were intense, boring into her very soul, so she pulled herself up straight and faced him with confidence.

'I am hungry,' she said, smiling, 'but I don't want to keep you if you have more important things to do.'

'I wouldn't have suggested it if I'd had another pressing engagement, Veronica. You seem to have settled in extremely well, even enjoying yourself, am I right?'

'Mm,' Veronica answered. She didn't want to sound too keen. 'Everyone here is so friendly—yes, I am enjoying my stay.'

'But you're keen to find your unknown family?' The lift stopped and the doctor led the way out and along the corridor into the cafeteria. 'Or is that a raw nerve? You seem to be reluctant to discuss it?'

'I don't want to hurt anyone, that's not my intention, Dr Linley.'

'Oliver, please—we're into first names here, as you've probably noticed, especially off duty.'

Veronica paused while they stood at the counter and ordered their choice of food, his a steak with french fries, and a side salad, but she preferred a fish and cheese dish with salad. The large, airy room was not over-crowded and she followed Oliver to a far corner near the window, away from everyone else. 'I may not be success-ful in finding anyone,' she said. 'But if I do, all I need say is that my mother knew of the family from my grand-mother way back during the war.'

'And you think that won't stir up a hornets' nest?' He pursed his lips and smiled almost scornfully. 'My dear Veronica, people aren't stupid. If they've never heard of you and your family don't you think they'll be instantly suspicious?'

'I'm trying not to think along those lines, in fact I must confess I'm trying not to think about the idea too much at all. It'll mean a trip to Rochester probably, and although I'd like to see more of the States while I'm here, travelling around is costly and there are more interesting places to visit.'

'Rochester is a nice town, and you could incorporate it with a visit to Niagara Falls, and Canada perhaps?'

'That would be lovely, I hadn't thought of that.'

'Travelling isn't much of a problem here, in spite of your unfortunate experience when you arrived. I can only apologise for Kennedy Airport, it's not usually that bad except when flights are delayed and several large groups of people descend on it all demanding attention, then utter chaos prevails, but you'll find when you go back there it's an easy place to travel from once you've found the right terminal. You should see New York and Washington, there's also the Grand Canyon, Disneyland, although it might be easier for you to go down to Orlando to see Disney World, exactly the same of course but a bit nearer than going across to the west coast.'

'I don't suppose I shall see half of what I'd like to—after all, I'm here to work,' Veronica reminded him.

'The hours are good and you get days off, you must see to it that do you see what you want to. I'd be much happier to think of you sightseeing than going off on wild goose chases.'

'I have to do what I came to do.'

A shadow fell across them and a large bulky frame leaned over the table. 'Mind if I join you? Or is this a private conversation?'

Veronica looked up into the boyish face of Dave Wilfroy. She was glad he had been in charge of Oliver's team in his absence because of his friendly manner. He had been helpful too, making her feel at home at once, and even in this short time she knew that their friendship was growing quite rapidly.

'I'm trying to get to know our new New England nurse,' said Oliver with only the hint of a smile. He didn't quite manage to hide his impatience at the intrusion, but Dave chose to ignore it. He sat down on one of the spare seats and began to tuck into his large meal, but there was a lot of him to fill, Veronica acknowledged with a secret smile. She had liked him from the start because of his openness and pleasant manner not only to her but to his patients as well. He was as tall as Oliver but much broader, with dark, hazel-coloured eyes and a full sensuous mouth, whereas Oliver had a more distinguished look about him. He was lean, with square shoulders and narrow hips, well-sculpted features and hair which, beside Dave's light blond hair, appeared much darker than in some lights. As yet she only knew Oliver by repute, but Dave was uncomplicated, a bachelor with a fondness for women but with no enthusiasm to embark on a serious relationship which might lead to marriage. Veronica didn't need to be told the score, she had met plenty of other similar types, so she could feel free to enjoy his easy friendship. Oliver was a man with principles, reliable to a fault and conscientious about his profession, or so she had been led to believe. She remembered having definite heady thoughts about the man who had come to her aid at Kennedy, apart from feeling grateful, and afterwards unable to get him out of her mind.

'She's an excellent nurse and a nice person to know,' said Dave. 'We're lucky to have her on our team.'

'I'm afraid I've taken her away from Outpatients, Dave,' said Oliver. 'We saw Mrs Walcott this morning and she's in room twelve now, ready for her op tomorrow morning, so I thought it would be good for Veronica to stick with the old lady. It's nice to see a case through, and Jenny Pearson is in as well, just down the corridor, so Veronica can keep her eye on them both.'

'Oh!' Dave paused with his fork halfway to his mouth. 'How did Natalie take that?'

'Not quite as amicably as I'd hoped, but she agreed in the end.'

'And Gloria?' Dave questioned.

'Only time will tell.'

'Shouldn't Veronica be warned?'

'I'm sure she's experienced enough to handle our Gloria.'

'You can't leave me in suspense now,' Veronica protested. 'Who's Gloria?'

'The nurse in charge of that floor. A little over-officious at times, but don't let that alarm you,' Oliver said.

Veronica felt her spirits sink. She had so far got on well with her colleagues, but she felt some apprehension now at what tomorrow might bring forth.

'I hope I'm not being a scapegoat,' she said as light-heartedly as she could. 'First you antagonise Natalie by moving me, and if it's going to offend this Gloria then why can't I stay where I am?'

'Because I want to please an old lady, and it will give you the opportunity of seeing how the theatre runs on well-oiled wheels.'

'I've always liked theatre work, I must admit, so I shall enjoy that experience.'

'Are you finding things much as you'd expected?' Oliver asked, but instead of waiting for her reply he turned at once to Dave and said: 'Wasn't it a strange coincidence, Dave? Veronica and I met at Kennedy when she had just arrived and I was leaving for home.'

'You remember I told you that a kind gentleman had intervened on my behalf?' Veronica reminded Dave.

'If only we'd known,' Oliver went on with a warm smile. 'I think we shall have to make better arrangements in the future for our exchange staff. Because of fog and the likelihood of other delays it isn't always easy to get up here to Groton just when you've planned, and being in a strange country can be frightening. Still, I think Veronica here was being very positive about it, even if she did threaten to turn around and go home.'

'Well, I'm glad she didn't,' said Dave with a saucy wink in Veronica's direction.

'We must have that team meeting as soon as possible, Dave.' Suddenly Oliver's voice was anything but friendly. 'I suppose as usual you're tied up this evening?' He looked at his watch significantly.

'Actually no,' said Dave. 'I've had a less strenuous day now that you're back, so I'd planned an early night, but it would be a good idea to get together as I need to put you in the picture about a few patients before I forget.'

'If you've kept your notes up to date then there shouldn't be any fear about you forgetting,' Oliver said curtly.

'It'll be easier to talk about them while they're fresh in my mind.' Dave didn't seem the slightest bit put out about Oliver's inference and he finished his meal and stood up, placing a hand on Veronica's back as he did so. 'See you around then, Veronica, in OR tomorrow morning.' He paused and looked at Oliver. 'And you in your office, Oliver, in fifteen minutes?'

'Something like that,' Oliver grunted in reply.
Veronica felt the atmosphere between the two men and
wondered about the situation, but Oliver laughed. 'Just
harmless baiting, Veronica,' he said. 'Dave is a good
doctor.' His brow puckered. 'Never slow to challenge a
new and pretty face, though, so be warned.'

'I like Dave,' Veronica said forcefully. 'He's been a
good colleague and eager to help.'

'Then perhaps he can help you find your folks. I'm
sure I can't really advise you if you've made up your
mind. You could save up so that at the end of the year
you have the resources to spend a month or so travelling
from state to state, or you can save up a couple of
weekends and have a few days off every three months or
so.'

'I certainly don't intend to let it interfere in any way
with my work schedule, Dr Linley, but for my mother's
sake I must try to trace her family,' Veronica said
earnestly.

She had been at the point of giving up the whole idea,
but Oliver Linley's persuasion to do that only served to
make her more determined. 'I'd better get home to bed
if I'm to be up early tomorrow,' she said as she stood up.
Oliver was instantly on his feet.

'I'm sure you're going to enjoy your year with us,
Veronica, whether you achieve your aim or not. If
there's anything I can do you have only to ask.' He
inclined his head and she took her bag from the back of
the chair and slung it over her shoulder. 'Thanks very
much, but for the immediate future it will have to be
done by correspondence, I think,' she said. With an
added 'Good night' she left the cafeteria and took the lift
down to the underground car-park.

It was still quite light and she drove the short distance
to the old Colonial house called Riverside where she and
several other nurses had small apartments. Dave and an
intern called Robert Olsen shared the ground floor,
which was supposed to be for the girls' protection,
though they were seldom at home. It was three storeys

high and Veronica had the top attic flat to herself, which
pleased her, while a caretaker and his wife lived in the
basement. The only drawback was the three flights of
twisting stairs which could be a daunting sight after a
hard day's work, but now after parking her car in her
allotted space at the side of the old house Veronica went
up to her own domain quite happily. She changed into
her jeans and a thin check shirt, then took from her bag
the letter which she had already composed to the War
Department. It read quite well, she decided, but a name
and an old Army number was hardly enough to find
someone after forty years. On the other hand, what did
she have to lose? She sealed it up and put the stamp on,
then with a moment's renewed misgivings stuffed it back
in her bag. Just a few more days, she decided, though
what she was waiting for she couldn't imagine!

At the nurses' station the next morning Veronica reported for duty to the nurse in charge, who was a tall,
large woman with a forbidding expression. Veronica
couldn't quite put her finger on why she considered the
older woman forbidding. Was it the size of her? Maybe
the dark olive skin and the jet black shiny hair? Or was
it just the way she glowered down at Veronica in
acknowledgement as Veronica introduced herself?

'I'm Veronica Summers, assigned to special Mrs
Walcott.'

Veronica thought there might have been a hint of
amusement flicker across Gloria Tucker's face, and in
that instant she had to admit that this forty-year-old
nurse was quite good-looking for her age, attractive in a
brooding kind of way.

'I don't know about specialling her,' Gloria said
almost contemptuously. 'And I don't know why Oliver
should think we need extra help, but you'll find the old
lady in room twelve. Surgery on a ninety-year-old—I
ask you!'

'I understand it's to help her digestive problem,'
Veronica said, trying to sound professional.

Gloria snorted her disgust. 'If I were her age I'd just

want to be left alone to die in peace.'

'It might be a very painful death. I don't suppose it will be much of an operation, just enough to make her more comfortable.'

'Have to hand it to the old girl, she's lived a good, useful life and she's mentally alert, but in my opinion the time and money should be spent on people at the other end of the scale with their lives before them.'

'Perhaps it's as well that Dr Linley doesn't see it that way,' Veronica dared to say.

Gloria's cheeks turned slightly darker, but she managed a smile as she said. 'Oh, Oliver will wear himself out for anyone of whatever age. You'd better go and attend to Mrs Walcott. She's first on the list and if she's not ready Oliver will raise Cain.'

Veronica noticed the change in attitude at the mention of Dr Linley's name, maybe an element of guilt too? Gloria accompanied Veronica to room twelve, where Mrs Walcott greeted them without any sign of nervousness.

'Hullo there, girls. Somehow I feel good today, maybe I don't need surgery after all?'

'That's because you've had nothing to eat,' said Gloria. 'Nothing to aggravate your system.' Veronica could hardly believe it was the same person speaking. Gloria was actually smiling, her eyes full of warm compassion towards Mrs Walcott, which seemed in complete contrast to everything she had just said. 'Dr Linley's found one of your own kith and kin to nurse you—that should please you?'

'It was very thoughtful of him, but you know very well, Nurse Tucker, that I'll never complain without good cause. Being in hospital isn't a pleasant experience at the best of times and when you get past ninety it's one you can do without, but I appreciate all that's being done and I know how hard you girls work. I'll try not to give you cause for alarm, and if I pop off I won't have wasted too much of your time.'

'Come on, Mrs Walcott, that's not the way you should be thinking,' chided Gloria. 'Just concentrate on how good it'll be to feel more comfortable when it's all over and you're home again.'

'If I ever get to my own home again,' the old lady snapped ungraciously. 'It's what I've got to go through first that worries me.'

'Veronica here is a fully trained nurse and she'll be taking special care of you, so you don't need to worry about a thing.'

Gloria Tucker placed her hands round Mrs Walcott's cheeks before saying to Veronica in a sickly sweet voice: 'The night staff have set up a trolley with all the preparations you'll need, so I'll leave you to it.'

Veronica wouldn't have been surprised if the senior nurse had stood over her to check that she was capable in her task, but fortunately she left the room and Veronica could continue with the normal procedure. When she helped Mrs Walcott into the gown and cap they laughed together easily at the old lady's: 'No chance of running away with these glad rags on!'

'Might start a new fashion,' Veronica suggested.

She found her patient submissive as she explained the reason why such preparations were necessary, and after the pre-med had been given Mrs Walcott soon became drowsy and uncommunicative.

Veronica was a little apprehensive as she walked beside the old lady on the trolley through the corridor and up in the lift to the suite of operating rooms. There seemed to be a great number of staff to-ing and fro-ing between the rooms, and a few eyebrows were raised as Veronica went into the changing room, leaving Mrs Walcott in the care of another nurse. She wondered how the rest of the staff would accept a new face in theatre. She hoped it wouldn't seem like favouritism to them, but an extra pair of hands anywhere was usually welcome. Robert Olsen was scrubbing up at the same time as Veronica.

'I'm doing this one under Oliver's watchful eye,' he whispered. 'I feel as uncertain as you look.'

'I'm only uncertain in that I'm wondering if I'm treading on anyone's toes by being here,' she told him. 'I love theatre work, did quite a long spell at home when I was a staff nurse.'

'You aren't likely to tread on anyone's toes, Veronica. As long as you're capable you'll be welcomed with open arms. I don't relish the thought of doing surgery on such an elderly lady, but Oliver assures me that she's a tough old bird.'

'How many ops have you done?' she asked.

'This will be my tenth. I'm an expert in appendicectomies and hernias, but this is a little more intricate, with the added worry of possible heart failure.'

'If that was a real problem surely surgery wouldn't be attempted?'

'No, so Oliver tells me. I've met Mrs Walcott in Outpatients and I know her condition, but I can't help but feel some misgivings.'

'Come along, you two, no time to stand gossiping!' Oliver made his presence felt by coming between Veronica and Robert. 'And you must stop feeling guilty about this one, Robert. If I had any doubts about her being able to withstand this op I wouldn't be allowing you to do it. Forget she's an old lady, think only of the fact that by taking out a piece of gut you're going to effect temporary relief. Her body is wearing out, no one can deny that, but our job is to lessen pain for anyone who's suffering. There are those who would rather administer nothing but drugs to relieve pain in a woman of this age, and she'd surely die from the effects of those drugs, so I prefer to do it my way.' He turned to face the rest of the team who were ready and waiting. 'One hundred per cent concentration, please, everyone, in support of Robert, and Mrs Walcott, who we all know is a very spirited and courageous lady.'

The anaesthetist put the patient into a deep sleep and her condition was monitored throughout, while Robert made the incision and removed a small length of gut. Veronica stood beside him ready with swabs and at first constantly wiping the sweat from his brow, but she watched his confidence grow, and the operation was carried out successfully with a minimum of fuss which earned the young surgeon Oliver's praise.

'Now it's over to you, Veronica,' said Oliver, as Mrs Walcott was wheeled away. 'The recovery room for the next few hours, then intensive care if required or back to room twelve. Robert did very well, didn't he? But you won't tell Mrs Walcott that I didn't do the op, will you?'

'I wouldn't dream of betraying you, Dr Linley,' Veronica said with a smile. 'I don't think Mrs Walcott will mind who did what when she begins to feel better.'

Oliver left her to retrace his steps, and Veronica thought how lucky Robert was to have such a kindly senior surgeon to work under. She could well remember the agony some young doctors went through when assigned to an older and occasionally tetchy consultant. Anger and frustration could cause chaos in theatre, but Oliver Linley seemed to be one who worked with quiet control. Yet she had considered that he was capable of impatience, she remembered, but maybe that was in his private relationships, it certainly wasn't evident in theatre. Gloria Tucker joined her in the recovery room later in the morning.

'How is she?' she asked with genuine concern.

'Fairly stable is all I can say at present.'

'How did it go? Did Oliver do all that he intended?'

'A piece of gut was inflamed and messy, so that's now been removed,' Veronica told her.

'Poor old soul. Seems a shame to put her through all this, doesn't it?'

'Let's hope she makes a quick recovery,' Veronica said. 'She's keen to get back home, so she appears to be the sort who will fight to do just that.'

'You'd best go for your break,' Gloria told her. 'I'll take over here.'

'Maybe I shall have time to look in on Jenny Pearson on my way back.'

'Yes, I understand Oliver had suggested that you keep an eye on her too. Better not tell Natalie. She likes to do the administering around here, especially where her nurses are concerned. Still, it's unlikely she'll quarrel with Oliver at present.'

'Why "at present"?' queried Veronica.

Gloria tilted her head to one side and with a sneering tone explained: 'My dear, you're competition. Natalie doesn't like new pretty faces in her domain, especially when the boss-man makes a point of requesting the pleasure of that pretty face at operations and to look after special cases.'

'I'm sure no one has any need to see me as "competition", as you put it. Dr Linley hardly knows me, but the fact that I'm English like he is just gives us something in common, I suppose.'

'I take it you're free of ties, otherwise you wouldn't have come over here to work for a year?'

'I'm free of domestic ties at last, which is why I came all this way to look for my mother's family, and no, I don't have any romantic ties at present, nor do I intend to get involved with anyone while I'm here. The most eligible bachelor at Brookville is perfectly safe from my claws, I can assure you.'

Veronica hurried away to the cafeteria, somewhat annoyed at Gloria's hints. She sat alone drinking piping hot coffee which brought a red glow to her cheeks and burned her tongue.

'By the way your lips are pressed together can I assume that you're peeved about something?' asked Natalie. She sat down at the vacant place next to Veronica and peered into her face. 'Not a good morning?' she asked.

'Workwise, excellent. Mrs Walcott is OK, thank goodness, and every moment that passes means more promise of a full recovery.'

'Not hitting it off with our Gloria, then?'

'She's—um—different, I suppose,' Veronica admitted.

'Don't you mean difficult?' Natalie asked.

'Actually no. We appear to be coping quite well, but I get the feeling that I'm looked upon as competition in the Oliver stakes?'

'Yes, well, he is rather popular—isn't any bachelor? And Gloria is forty, after all.'

'Is there anything between her and Oliver, or any
other member of the staff?' asked Veronica. 'After all,
I'd rather know so that I can avoid upsetting anyone.'

'Oliver is completely free and welcomes anyone who
can keep Gloria off his back. He likes harmony between
the staff. It's his hospital, he's the director, and he
doesn't have the time for personal relationships. Gloria
likes to think of herself as his protector, but she only
succeeds in embarrassing him. Oliver and I are old
friends, nothing more, in case Gloria has given you to
understand I regard him as my property. I wish he'd get
married and stop all the rumours and speculation. Don't
get me wrong, he likes women, but somehow I don't
think he'd ever get involved with anyone from the
hospital. He goes down to Florida sometimes, so he
could well have a special girlfriend down there.'

Natalie chattered on, but Veronica found herself
visualising the handsome Oliver coming off the plane in
Orlando or Miami with an armful of flowers to greet
the girl in question. She couldn't quite understand why
there was suddenly an empty ache in the pit of her
stomach . . .

Mrs Walcott was back in room twelve when Veronica
returned to duty. She had regained consciousness but
during the afternoon slept, sometimes peacefully, sometimes restlessly, frequently mumbling, and when she did
wake she was confused, which was as anticipated.

It was nearing the time for Veronica to go off duty
when she noticed the patient's laboured breathing, so
she gave her oxygen, and the sudden rise in temperature
and pulse rate alerted Veronica to report the change
immediately to Gloria.

'This is what you get in elderly people,' Gloria
grumbled as they lifted Mrs Walcott higher against a
mountain of pillows.

Veronica ignored Gloria's griping and persuaded the
old lady to breathe deeply and cough in order to remove
the plug of mucus which she suspected was blocking a
bronchus. By the time the physiotherapist arrived

a violent fit of coughing had brought relief, with the patient's temperature and pulse rate falling dramatically.

'I expected to find a doctor here,' Lorenza, the physiotherapist, said. 'You've paged Dr Linley, I take it?'

'No. He's got a long list today, after his holiday, so I'm sure he won't want to be disturbed.'

'Oh, come on, Gloria, you know better than that.' Gloria shrugged. 'Still, it's your floor, but you realise that I must include this in my report? Be prepared for an explosion!'

This didn't seem to worry Gloria, and eventually the other two girls left the room, while Veronica comforted Mrs Walcott as best she could but knowing that antibiotics should be given as soon as possible. It was necessary for a doctor to write a prescription for these, but the time came for her to go off duty and no one came. Veronica had assumed when the physiotherapist had been sent for that automatically a doctor would have been paged at the same time, and she was surprised that a nurse in charge hadn't done so. At home she would have made such decisions herself, but being on loan as it were to Brookville she couldn't override Gloria Tucker's authority. She made last-minute checks on her patient and prepared to leave, but raised voices coming through the corridor made her pause. Oliver burst into the room.

'I thought you were fully experienced and well qualified to deal with cases like Mrs Walcott!' he stormed.

'I'm not in charge here, Dr Linley,' she replied calmly. 'At home I was in a position where I made the decisions myself, but here I did the next best thing and reported Mrs Walcott's condition to the head nurse.

'But it never occurred to you that it should have been reported to *me*?' His handsome face was dark with anger, the strain of several hours' surgery clearly visible in his furrowed brow. 'You only had to pick the phone up, for God's sake!'

'I attended to my patient, *and* succeeded in relieving her distress,' Veronica said with as much dignity as she could salve. 'I'm not familiar with procedure here on the wards as yet—and *I'm* not in charge.'

'*I* put you in charge of Mrs Walcott, and that covers everything relating to her care.' The large room seemed stifled of air as Oliver faced Gloria. 'Is that understood?'

'Why, sure—that's exactly what I presumed you meant,' she replied smugly.

Veronica stared at her, flushing at the smile of self-satisfaction that triumphed on the head nurse's face.

'I didn't presume as much,' Veronica cut in with a bite. 'Being qualified is one thing, being given instant responsibility on someone else's floor quite unusual. Especially,' she added pointedly, 'in an unfamiliar hospital in a strange country.'

'Are you saying you can't handle it?' Oliver enquired.

'No, I'm not saying that, Dr Linley—just so long as I know where I stand.'

'Total responsibility for Mrs Walcott during your hours of duty—understood?'

Veronica nodded, then as Oliver turned to go she said: 'You'll have written up for antibiotics, of course?'

'Of course nothing—as yet I haven't been asked.' He turned with a questioning frown to Gloria, who smiled sweetly with an expression of 'poor Dr Linley, *so* over-worked', but she said: 'The old lady did recover quite dramatically, doctor, and antibiotics aren't always advisable for the elderly.'

'With the right treatment, Nurse Tucker, people do recover frequently,' he said sarcastically. 'Elderly or not, they have as much right to first class care as you have.' He turned to Veronica again and gave her instructions as to the dosage for the antibiotics he prescribed. 'Veronica looks as if she's about to go off duty so, Nurse Tucker, will you see that these tablets are obtained at once and pass on the instructions to the night staff, please.'

When he had gone Gloria heaved a sigh of relief. 'Lot of fuss about nothing!' She went to look at the charts

hanging at the end of the bed and then with some private
mutterings of her own she left the room. Veronica had
no intention of embarking on a slanging match with her,
even though she felt she had been discredited unjustly.

Mrs Walcott barely opened her eyes when Veronica
squeezed her hand and wished her a restful night. The
next forty-eight hours would be crucial, but with the old
lady's determination and Veronica's encouragement she
prayed that this particular case would be successful.

Veronica went off duty a short time later with a
mixture of emotions. She had felt like throwing in the
towel, but she couldn't afford to come all this way and
find herself without a job, and even worse, without
somewhere to live. No, she must put up with Gloria's
lack of perfection and simply prove that she herself was
competent in her profession.

On reaching Riverside she let herself into her top flat
and securely chained the door. She could have done with
some fresh air. A walk by the river would have helped to
clear her brain of her frustration, but instead she had a
shower and went to bed with the book she was reading.
She didn't turn any pages, though, for in her mind's eye
was the anger in Oliver's face and the look of victory in
Gloria's expression. The woman was jealous of her
presence at Brookville, let alone Veronica being given
precedence over her in a special case. Whatever motive
could Oliver have had in suggesting such a thing? It
seemed everyone knew of Gloria's attitude. The rest
of the staff treated Veronica with such warm friendliness
and she had really enjoyed her first few weeks at
Brookville; she did hope that things weren't going to
become awkward now. Shortly afterwards the book fell
with a thud to the floor, but she couldn't be bothered to
pick it up, instead she tried to shut out all other intru-
sions, and snuggling into the pillow was soon asleep.

CHAPTER THREE

WHEN Veronica reached Brookville next morning only one other nurse was in the locker room and after a brief exchange of polite conversation she reported for duty. Mrs Walcott had slept reasonably well with no further breathing disturbances, according to the night nurse. Certainly she had a little more colour, Veronica found when she went along to room twelve.

'How do you feel this morning?' Veronica asked, but before she got an answer Oliver Linley walked briskly into the room.

'Good morning, Veronica,' he said softly, then went straight to his patient's bedside. 'And how's my favourite girl today? Feeling better, I hope?'

'All the better for seeing you, young man,' the old lady croaked goodhumouredly.

Oliver smiled in a disarming way, picked up her chart, studied it briefly, replaced it and moved a step closer to Veronica. 'Any observations?' he asked.

'I've hardly had time, I've only just arrived.'

'I'll come back later to see Mrs Walcott, and hope you've woken up by then,' he said, tapping her shoulder lightly as he slid behind her and left the room.

Veronica felt his visit had been a waste of time, or had it been deliberately to see how she had reacted to the trouble the previous day? To her surprise Mrs Walcott pulled herself up gently and smiled at her. 'What was all the fuss about yesterday? I know I felt as if I were dying, but I feel much better this morning.'

Veronica explained with only the briefest of details about why Mrs Walcott had breathing problems. 'You responded well, and did as I asked, so that we soon had everything under control,' she told her.

'Sounded like someone was getting the sharp end of

Dr Linley's tongue, and that's not like him. I hope it wasn't you, my dear?'

'Just a conflict of ideas, Mrs Walcott. I don't think it was such a good idea having me come to look after you. I'd already been assigned to Outpatients, so Natalie wasn't too pleased, and I'm sure Gloria thinks that by putting me on her floor Dr Linley is undermining her ability. It's nothing of the sort really. I'm here to help out wherever an extra pair of hands is required. I don't mind where I work.'

'That Gloria Tucker would have been quite happy if I'd popped off,' said the old lady, 'but Dr Linley would have worried about his reputation and that of Brookville. It's the best hospital there is around here and he's known for his kindness to young and old alike.'

'Your welfare is all we're concerned about,' Veronica assured Mrs Walcott, patting the frail, blue-veined hand.

'Yes, my dear, I know you're doing your best, and most of the staff. After all, they could have left me at home to die. I can't have that much longer to live, but Gloria probably thinks I should have been helped on my way.'

'Now, none of that,' Veronica said firmly. 'You're going to be fine. It wasn't a big operation, just a little blockage removed, but even that's bound to make you feel sore for a while. Does your chest feel easier now?'

Mrs Walcott nodded. 'My own fault for being a smoker all my life.' She managed a weak smile. 'Haven't done so bad, though, have I?'

'You're a survivor,' Veronica smiled. 'I'll just take your temperature and give you your pills, then you can settle down for a real sleep.'

'You watch out for that Gloria Tucker,' Mrs Walcott warned. 'She'll find a way of showing you in a bad light in front of Dr Linley if she can. I know her sort, and I know how every woman in Brookville, married or not, would love to take him home to supper.' In spite of any discomfort she was feeling Mrs Walcott winked saucily at Veronica.

'I think you're going to talk your way out of here very shortly,' Veronica laughed. 'But how come you know so much about the staff here?'

'Better come clean, I suppose. Gloria Tucker and me are old acquaintants. Her family lived right next door to me at one time when she was a schoolgirl. Nice enough folks, but money split the family. Sad, that was. I don't know why Gloria took to nursing. Her father would have helped her into something more glamorous that was less hard work, but I'll say that for her, she's stuck by her mother. Reckon she could be bitter because no man has as yet whisked her off to the altar, but there's still time for a sick millionaire to come along. She's wasting her time drooling over Dr Linley, though. He has the charm to pick the girls up and the cool nerve to drop 'em right down again.'

Veronica laughed this off, but she was glad to hear any snippets of gossip about the handsome Oliver Linley. Later on in the morning when Mrs Walcott had slept for a couple of hours Veronica took her along to the shower room, one with a cork seat especially designed for the elderly, and after that she sat out in a chair near the large picture window. When the drinks trolley came round the old lady chose tea to drink but refused anything to eat, so Veronica was able to go for her own break, leaving another nurse to watch Mrs Walcott.

While she was enjoying her coffee Dave Wilfroy came in to join her.

'Hello, gorgeous,' he greeted her cheerfully. 'How's things?'

They went into a casual conversation about the previous day's events and the condition of Mrs Walcott.

'Lots of girls hate geriatric cases,' said Veronica, 'but Mrs Walcott is so mentally alert. She hates being a bother to anyone, but she loves a good gossip.'

'Well, how about us going off somewhere and giving the gossips something to whet their appetite?' Dave suggested with a boyish grin. 'You should be having a day off shortly, or the weekend?'

'It sounds a lovely idea, Dave, but I've got to decide what to do about finding my mother's father.'

'Oh yes, that.' He looked away, down into the contents of his cup, and Veronica felt the atmosphere change.

'You don't approve? Do you think I'll be stirring up a hornets' nest, as Oliver put it?'

'Mm . . . it isn't for me to approve or disapprove, is it? It must be your decision, Veronica, but it's going to take a great deal of your time for one thing. I was hoping we'd be spending our off duty together, as much as we can arrange, that is.'

Veronica felt her cheeks colour slightly. She liked Dave a lot and her fantasies had included him, but now that Oliver had intruded into her life she found she didn't want to become involved too deeply with anyone else. She knew she was being foolish. As if Oliver cared a jot for her—but there was something in his enigmatic smile and the way his blue eyes surveyed her which made her vulnerable where he was concerned. At twenty-five she had begun to think that a serious relationship was out of the question. Men of her age and older seemed so set in their ways that marriage wasn't attractive, but for Veronica it was what she dreamed of. That didn't mean she didn't enjoy the work. It usually came first, which was why previous boyfriends took off when they found that her duty hours were rather too flexible—flexible to suit either the hospital or her patients, but never to suit them! She had resolved not to let work interfere in a relationship again since the death of her mother and the release from looking after her father. She wondered how Ellie was getting on. Any minute she expected to get a cable to say that she was on her way to Groton as well. Veronica knew that her father would have preferred it to be Ellie who was getting the benefit of a year in America, but her mother had specifically asked Veronica to go, and it was more easily arranged than for Ellie, who had no particular job experience. She found Dave's suggestion complimentary, but refused to give up all ideas of her quest even for him.

'That sounds very pleasant,' she answered non-committally, 'but I mustn't lose sight of the reason I'm here.'

'Have you sent that letter off yet?'

Veronica sighed. 'No, not yet. Something seems to be holding me back. I want to get on with it—after all, what am I going to tell my father when I ring or write? I suppose it's just cold feet—you know, delving into the unknown, and then Oliver thought it was a mistake, so here I am with nothing to show for my first month in the States—still,' she laughed, 'I've got all of eleven months left.'

'And we mustn't waste another minute of it.' Dave reached out and clasped her hand in his. Veronica felt a cold shiver run down her back. Not from distaste, but just when she had thought she could easily form a more lasting relationship she knew that this was not the right man. She hoped she hadn't encouraged Dave, but in her heart she knew she hadn't done anything to dissuade him either.

'Dave,' she began, 'it isn't sensible to get too involved, is it?'

'I don't see why not.' Then he nodded and let go her hand. 'OK, I get the drift. I'm moving too fast. But I must admit it didn't seem like that a few days ago.'

'It's just that I don't want you to get the wrong idea about me. I like you a lot, and you've made me feel at home here. I enjoy going out with you and I hope we can continue to be friends.'

'But a good night kiss is all that's permissible?' He held up his hands in surrender. 'You won't blame me for persevering, will you?'

Veronica laughed, hoping he would see their friendship in a none-too-serious vein, but at that moment she was paged and immediately hurried back to the ward, thinking that perhaps Mrs Walcott hadn't been as tough as everyone thought. When she reported to the nurses' station Gloria looked up and even managed a smile.

'Dr Linley would like to see you in his office downstairs,' she said.

Veronica raised her eyebrows and returned to the lift, but this time going down. She found Oliver's door half open, but she knocked positively and walked in.

'Ah, Veronica, come in,' he said, and walked behind her to close the door. Now what had she done wrong? she wondered, but he indicated that she should sit in the easy chair opposite him. 'I just wanted you to know that I was very impressed with your performance yesterday. Your instant reaction probably saved Mrs Walcott's life. A more junior nurse might well have panicked. I suppose I ought to apologise for Gloria—well, she should do so herself, but pride won't let her. I realise I've put you in a very awkward situation, one that Gloria will agree with in principle because I say she must, but she won't make things easy for you. Now, how do you feel about it? I want you to be perfectly honest, and if you feel it puts you under too much strain then by all means go back to Outpatients, or wherever Natalie needs you.'

'And give Gloria the satisfaction of knowing I couldn't take working under her? Oh no, Dr Linley, you asked me to look after Mrs Walcott and I want to see it through.'

His blue eyes twinkled across at her almost wickedly. 'Good for you! Yes, I believe you can hold your own, but if she gets too much then will you promise me that you'll come and tell me? After all, we don't want you going home at the end of the year giving us a bad report.'

'I certainly shan't do that.'

'I . . . I feel I ought to make it up to you in some way, Veronica.'

'Why ever should you feel that?' she asked in surprise. 'It's over now, and I hope Mrs Walcott will make it, at least for some while yet.'

Oliver sighed and shook his head. 'I never met a gutsier lady,' he said. 'But none of us can live for ever and she's outlived her three score years and ten. I'm glad you're going to continue caring for her, she'll be glad too. I . . . I wondered if you'd allow me to take you out to supper, or for the day perhaps,' he added, 'show you around—that's if Dave hasn't already claimed all your days off.'

Veronica felt herself going weak at the knees. Now, steady! she told herself. This is only his way of apologising for being hasty yesterday—but she couldn't let such a golden opportunity go by, could she?

'That's very kind of you—but really there's no need,' she began, hating herself for not being able to answer honestly.

The 'telling' smile was back, which made her feel quite pleased that she had not jumped at the golden opportunity.

'I daresay I'm not quite as debonair as our Dave,' said Oliver, now smiling broadly, 'but I don't think I'm bad company either. At least I can show you things which perhaps interest us as being British.'

'It's much nicer to be shown around than trying to find my own way, though Americans are very hospitable,' Veronica agreed.

'When are you due a day off then?'

'Not until the weekend.'

'Ah, that's good, but I suppose you're planning on a wild goose chase?'

'No, not until I've got some more information to go on. But I can't impose on your weekend, Oliver.'

'It'll be a pleasure, and I'll try to arrange something interesting.'

'I shall look forward to it. About Mrs Walcott—she's feeling quite comfortable and her condition is stable.'

Oliver cast his eyes downwards then slowly back to meet her gaze. 'I don't have any real doubts about your capabilities, Veronica, even though Gloria may be tempted to try to put you down. Just keep alert to any little games she may try, though having been found out once she isn't likely to do it again. She's a good nurse, but her home life isn't easy and she tends to let frustration rule her head. Unfortunately she sees every younger nurse or patient as a threat. Silly woman,' he muttered, 'but I can't be held responsible if she tries to outdo any of her colleagues. It's up to all of you to be one jump ahead of her.'

'I'll be on my guard now that I know how she can react, but I'm sure we shall get on all right,' Veronica assured him. 'I haven't had a chance to visit Jenny Pearson yet—any further developments?'

'Not anything significant. I'm waiting for the results of the tests we've run, and meanwhile she's resting and being persuaded to eat more sensibly. She doesn't have any visitors because all her friends are down in New Haven, so she says, but I can't help feeling there must be someone around this area who knows her. I have to be careful, because if I pry she may well get the wrong impression, and I don't want to add to her problems.'

'She did tell me a little bit about herself—about how she looked after her mother, and after she died there was a man friend whom she obviously became very fond of until she found out that he was married. He wanted to continue the affair, but she'd have none of that. It must have taken some courage to continue working at the same place that he did, but then she finally went down to New Haven to a new job, and now she can't decide whether or not to sell up her home and go down there to live permanently.'

'You've done very well to discover that much, Veronica. Encourage her to talk as openly as possible so that if there's anyone around here who's interested we can drop a discreet hint that she could do with a visitor. She's suffering from fear and loneliness, and that's not right in one so young.'

'Once she begins to feel stronger she should be able to cope with her social life,' she said.

'It's her love life I'm worried about,' Oliver confessed. 'She looks at me as if she could devour me. She's a nice kid, but I can't show her anything more than professional interest.'

'I'm sure she doesn't expect you to, but no one can prevent her from dreaming.'

Oliver raised his eyebrows in his usual meaningful manner. 'I'm eager to see her walk out of here strong and well, with or without dreams about whoever. Keep me or Dave informed, Veronica. We must just do the best we can for her.' He stood up and pushed his hands deep into his side pockets. 'I look forward to Saturday and Sunday. I hope you aren't the sort who needs to sleep on when you don't have to come to work?'

Veronica laughed. 'I'm well trained to wake early when I have to.'

'We can make an early start, then, let's hope for good weather.' He walked her to the door, and she returned to the lift happily anticipating the weekend, but wondering what other people were going to think. What was Dave going to say? Was she being disloyal? But no, she had as good as told him that there couldn't be anything serious in their relationship. She hoped he wouldn't be suspicious, but he had already realised that her attitude had changed since Oliver's return. She sighed thoughtfully, wishing friendships with the opposite sex didn't have to be so complicated.

For the next two days Mrs Walcott slept a great deal, which gave Veronica time to meet other patients on that floor, and she frequently stopped by Jenny's room for a chat. The younger girl was still scared that she wasn't being told the truth about her condition, but at last the test results came through, and Oliver spent over an hour with Jenny explaining in great detail how she had got herself into such a state and how she could help herself. It was Friday afternoon and Veronica was just going off duty to prepare herself for the weekend when Oliver came to look for her.

'Oh dear, are you just off?' he asked.

'Yes, but I'm not in a hurry,' she said.

'I'd be grateful if you could spend half an hour with Jenny to back me up. She nods her head in agreement, but I can see that she doesn't really trust me, and she's ready for a weep. She won't let herself go in front of me. Be a dear and see what you can do, Veronica.' Oliver walked a few paces beside her, then with his hand hovering somewhere in the vicinity of her right hip he whispered: 'I'll pick you up at Riverside at nine o'clock tomorrow morning.'

She smiled up at him and went into Jenny's room, quite unprepared for what she found. Jenny was dressed and standing by the bed, her suitcase open ready to accept the belongings she was about to throw into it. She faced Veronica aggressively. 'So,' she said angrily, 'now that you've had your fun at my expense I can go home and die at mine!'

'Jenny! What are you talking about? There's no question of you going home yet. Dr Linley has been trying to explain that there's nothing seriously wrong with you and that with rest and care you'll soon be fit again.'

'You must take me for a fool! I've never been fit—ever—and I know I'm going to die, so just let me get on with it. I've had it up to here with platitudes!' Jenny lifted her hand to her chin, then in the ensuing silence she glanced at Veronica, her eyes filling, her chin quivering before she gave way to a deluge of tears.

Veronica did her best to console the girl, giving her tissues, replacing her belongings in the drawers and closing the suitcase, and as she put it back on top of the wardrobe she said: 'Jenny, you're in no fit state to go home yet, but that still doesn't mean that there's any disease. Trust us, please. I promise you you'll be able to go home in the future feeling very differently from how you do now.'

Jenny lay across the bed, her slim body shaking violently from the awful sobs which exhausted her. Veronica was moved with compassion. If she had been left alone in the world, no Ellie, no father to share each other's grief, this could be how she might have felt—isolated, frightened, unloved.

'Jenny, there must be someone who cares about you,' Veronica said softly. 'An aunt, a cousin, a friend?'

Jenny shook her head vigorously. 'No one,' she said, 'and please don't keep on at me. I . . . I can't take any more.' She continued to weep, and Veronica gathered up the things on her locker, but before she placed them in the drawer she noticed a security card in an outside pocket of her purse, the details visible through clear plastic, bearing a photo of Jenny, a number and the name of the firm she worked for. She didn't need to look for many seconds before she had the firm's name indelibly registered in her brain. How much did her employers know of her illness? This was something she could discuss with Oliver tomorrow. When the room was tidy again Veronica persuaded Jenny to sit near the window.

'Oh dear, the weather looks as if it's about to break,' she said. 'Just because I'm off for the weekend. Look at that black cloud! Does that mean days and days of storms?'

'Not necessarily,' Jenny actually laughed. 'Evidently you haven't been here long enough to have heard the saying, "Wait until five o'clock and the sun will come out"—I don't know why it's true, but it does seem to be!'

'I hope you're right. It's been so lovely for the past few weeks, much more humid than at home, but beautifully warm.'

'If you're going to be here for the winter then be prepared for a complete contrast.' Jenny shivered, and by her wan cheeks Veronica knew that she had suddenly gone very cold.

'I'll go and get us a cup of tea,' she said. 'I'm due for a break, so I may as well have it with you.'

'You don't have to be nice to me, Veronica. I don't deserve it, and I'm sure Dr Linley would wash his hands of me if he'd heard me carrying on at you. I'm sorry, Veronica, it was unforgivable. I think I know, somewhere deep inside me, that you're right, but then I get to thinking about my mother and all the old doubts creep in until I'm convinced all over again that I've got the same as she had. It isn't feasible, after all, if I had I'd be much worse by now, probably dead.'

'You're better, and you must keep telling yourself that, Jenny. You really do have more colour in your cheeks than at the beginning of the week. The iron pills, the vitamins we've given you have given you a boost, but our minds govern a great deal of how our bodies behave, you know.'

'Yes, I do know. I've tried to get into this healthy mind, healthy body attitude. I guess some of my trouble is my job,' Jenny admitted.

'Oh? What makes you say that? I thought you enjoyed your work?'

'I do, but—well, I seem to lack confidence. Everyone is new and I don't make friends easily. After—the trouble with Mark—I find it difficult to trust anyone. It's so silly, because the people are very nice and most seem genuine.'

'It was a big step to take, moving jobs and going to a different town after losing your mother, but it'll work out all right in the end.'

Veronica went away to fetch the tea, glad that at least she had calmed Jenny down and pleased that the girl had opened up enough to talk about her fears. When she returned to the room some ten minutes later Jenny was standing looking out at the rain which was coming down in sheets, but Veronica was quick to notice that she had mopped up her tears and even put on a light make-up. That was a good sign, so she settled herself for a further half hour or so to be company for Jenny. She poured the tea and handed her patient a plate on which there was an enormous piece of coffee gateau. Jenny's eyes lit up in surprise.

'Heavens!' she exclaimed. 'Where on earth did you find this? Not an advertisement for healthy eating! And you're going to indulge too?'

'It'll save me from having afternoon tea when I get home. Probably a bad English custom anyway! Naughty but nice. It seemed such a shame to leave it on the counter in the cafeteria, and I don't fancy driving home in this storm anyway.'

Even as Veronica spoke lightning flashed across the sky and shortly afterwards thunder shook the atmosphere. Jenny appeared not to be disturbed, but Veronica felt her stomach begin to churn. She hated thunderstorms, had done ever since she could remember, and no amount of consoling could help her to overcome her fear, but she endeavoured not to show

Jenny that she was nervous.

'Tell me about your work,' she invited between mouthfuls of sponge and coffee cream. 'Do you work alone or with a room full of people?'

'With two men mostly. Pinter's is a large firm and at least I'm lucky in that I'm well qualified with computers. I seem to get on with machines better than with people.' Jenny stuffed more cake into her mouth, saying: 'I adore walnuts!' This was quite obvious to Veronica, and she quietly marvelled at the change in Jenny from half an hour earlier. But was she anorexic? Would she make herself sick the moment Veronica had left? Veronica stayed on while the storm raged outside. It was better for Jenny to have company, so she asked as many questions as was prudent about the firm Jenny worked for while between them they emptied the pot of tea.

'I know you're only here because you were afraid I was going to run off,' Jenny said, avoiding answering Veronica's question. 'But you're scared of thunder and lightning, aren't you?'

'That wasn't kind, Jenny,' Veronica protested goodhumouredly. 'I hoped it didn't show, but yes, I'm not ashamed to admit it, I'm terrified, especially when I'm alone.'

'I suppose that's not often?' said Jenny.

'Hardly ever, at home. I'm lucky I have some family, but here I have a small apartment to myself, so I shall have to hide under the bedclothes when there's a storm. It's always easier to be brave in company.'

'For me it's the other way around. I'm a real coward in company. I was so used to just Mum and myself being on our own for most of the time. I like being on my own, and I prefer working alone, but that's something I can't choose. The other two guys aren't bad, they have each other and as yet take very little notice of me. I suppose in a way I'm dreading getting better because of having to return to work. It'll be like starting all over again.'

'You've just faced up to a problem by airing it, Jenny,' Veronica told her. 'That's good, now when the time comes it won't seem nearly so bad. I'm sure there must be other single women there who would be friendly.'

'It's not the kind of work where I have a lot to do with other people, and in the staff canteen I tend to sit alone. I even choose a time when the place will be uncrowded, it suits me better that way.'

'Have you never had any contact with your father, Jenny?'

As soon as Veronica had voiced the question she regretted it. From the dark frown which changed Jenny's expression she guessed that this might be the clue to her emotional problem, but Jenny's face cleared quickly and she shrugged. 'Nope,' she said uninterestedly. 'And I don't want to.'

'But whoever he is, Jenny, he is your father, your next of kin, and he'd probably love to get to know you.'

'Well, he isn't going to, and that's that!'

Veronica realised that this was one area she must avoid, so she picked up the tray and went to look out at the weather.

'Thank goodness the storm seems to have passed. I'd best be on my way, but I've enjoyed your company, Jenny, and look, the sun's coming out!'

'What did I tell you? It's just turned five o'clock!'

The two girls laughed, and Veronica went on her way quite satisfied with the little she had gleaned from Jenny. So there was a father somewhere, and Jenny knew more than she was prepared to reveal.

When she reached Riverside she felt she should have been in a whirl of excitement, but she couldn't get Jenny out of her mind. She wished she could persuade her to talk more of her father and the reasons he left home. They could share in their respective quests, Jenny to look for her father, and Veronica to search for her grandfather. She remembered her letter still unposted. She'd never make any headway if she didn't do something soon, but tomorrow she was to have Oliver all to herself. She considered showing him her letter and enlisting his help, but dismissed this idea as he hadn't appeared to be very enthusiastic. No, tomorrow she

wanted to enjoy the day while she had the opportunity,
he might not like her enough to invite her out again!

Veronica slept fitfully and was quite unprepared for
the sound of the doorbell pealing urgently before she
was in proper control of herself. She pushed her arms
into her towelling robe, but one sleeve was inside out
and she couldn't quite get it right before the bell pealed
again. Oliver was much too early, but when she did get
to the door it was to find Dave standing with his arm
propped up against the doorjamb.

'Sorry, honey, I know I'm a poor substitute, but
Oliver . . .'

CHAPTER FOUR

VERONICA felt as if she had received a physical blow. She wanted to protest, but Dave looked so apologetic that she heard herself saying; 'Hullo, Dave. What did you say?'

'I can see you're not properly awake, though Oliver assured me that you'd be up and raring to go. I understand he was to take you out sightseeing for the weekend?'

'I don't know about for the weekend, but today, yes. He seemed keen to show me what he considers interesting.' She laughed lamely. 'Probably wouldn't have been much fun anyway.' She felt the disappointment so acutely that a pain shot across her forehead, making her eyes burn uncomfortably. She wasn't a good liar, but she hoped she was fooling Dave.

He pushed his way into her flat and closed the door behind him.

'Sorry, Veronica, I know you must be very disappointed, but something has come up and Oliver has to be at the hospital today.'

'Nothing wrong with any of our patients, I hope?'

'Nothing like that. A special brain surgeon is coming up from Orlando who Oliver must see, so he asked me to convey his apologies and says he'll make it on your next weekend off.'

Veronica ran her hand through her hair. 'He needn't bother,' she mumbled.

Dave laughed. 'You know you don't mean that,' he said. 'It's understandable that he's taken a shine to you since you're from his home country, but I daresay you feel like all the girls do about our Dr Linley. You can't kid me, Veronica. I hate having to inflict myself on you, but we've had some good times, so what do you say to trying to make the best of a bad job?'

'It's early yet. I certainly wasn't expecting Oliver at this time.'

'He said nine o'clock—OK, so it's barely half past eight, but as I live on the doorstep I thought I'd better come and tell you about the change of plan before you—well—you know.'

'No, Dave, I don't know what you're implying. I was preparing for a day out sightseeing—I didn't intend to dress up to impress.'

Dave turned her round and pushed her back into the bedroom. 'A cup of strong coffee—oh no, I see you've put the teapot and teabags ready, mind if I join you?'

'Be my guest,' Veronica replied, none too graciously.

'Get back into bed, then we can start all over again,' he said with a boyish grin, and switched on the small kettle which was on her bedside table. He went out to the kitchen and fetched milk from the fridge while Veronica went to the bathroom and splashed her face with cold water, then combed her hair before returning to her bedroom.

'You don't have to get up yet,' Dave said seriously. 'I'll go away and come back whenever you say.'

'Once I'm up, I'm up, and it's silly to waste any time in bed. Let's go into the kitchen. I don't suppose you've had any breakfast, so you may as well share mine.'

Dave carried the tray and Veronica switched on the toaster. 'Not much to offer, I'm afraid, and I expect you'd prefer coffee rather than tea?'

'Tea will suit me just fine, Veronica, and a piece of toast. I have a sizeable appetite, but later in the day suits me best.' Dave hovered behind her for a few minutes. 'I don't know what Oliver had planned, but I thought a trip up to Norwich to the park would be nice, or have you been there?'

'No. I've spent most of my off-duty getting used to this locality up to now. Dave, I'm sure you had something else planned for today, like seeing your parents perhaps?'

Dave shook his head. 'No, actually I'll be spending the day with them tomorrow. I should have taken my laundry to be done and shopped and cleaned, but that can wait. I'd hoped we'd be doing something together today until Oliver said he was taking charge of you.'

'When he asked me out I didn't know what to say. It would have been rude of me to refuse.'

'You don't have to make excuses to me, Veronica. You told me the score and I know things between us changed since Oliver returned. I . . . I guessed this would happen, so I got in quickly while he was away.'

'I'm beginning to wonder whether I should accept his offer,' she said, smiling at Dave, with whom she was very much at home. 'He sounds like a real Casanova.'

Dave was thoughtful while he chewed on his toast. 'Oliver likes women, they fall at his feet, but he has a definite idea of the ideal woman, and as soon as we saw you, red brown hair and soft dove-like eyes, I knew no one else would get a look in.' He continued chewing with concentration. 'But he isn't a man to get serious, Veronica. He's ambitious and he wants to move on, make a name for himself—medicine's like that here, there's a great deal of competition, so I doubt if a woman in his life can be a permanent arrangement. I may be quite wrong,' he added. 'Oliver isn't the kind of man you can ask such personal questions, but I feel it's kindest to warn you.'

'I'm not looking for a permanent involvement, Dave. I came here to work while I look for my grandfather or his family. I'm getting involved with my patients, Jenny for instance, and I'm enjoying it all, so you needn't be alarmed that I'll lose my head entirely.'

'From all that you've told me about your family and how devoted you all are, I wasn't really concerned, but I know Oliver's the type of man who can make a woman behave quite irrationally. Look at Gloria, for instance. She knew as well as I did that she should have paged Oliver the moment there was a change in Mrs Walcott's condition, but she just couldn't resist the opportunity of making you look incapable in his eyes. When he'd calmed down he saw it for himself, of course, and gave her a warning, but she needs this job, she has an ageing mother to provide for, and mostly she's a darned good nurse. You'd treated the old lady and done all that Oliver could have, so he had to admit that Gloria prevented him from being called away unnecessarily.'

'He said he felt I'd been judged wrongly, so asking me out was his way of apologising, even though he admitted it was Gloria's place to do that. He probably won't bother now, and I hope I shall soon be trotting off to Rochester on my next weekend off.'

Dave didn't reply, and Veronica was aware of a stifling atmosphere. He was too cute for her, he knew she was feeling bitterly disappointed that Oliver had let her down, but she would get over it, and probably realise it was for the best. While they finished their breakfast Veronica told Dave all that had passed between her and Jenny the previous day. He listened patiently with interest, then said: 'Pinter's is a good firm. They take real good care of their staff. I wonder just how much their personnel officer knows about Jenny. It might be worth following up.'

'I wondered about that, but we can't really interfere, can we? She'd do her nut, Dave,' Veronica protested.

'We'd have to be discreet, but there are ways round that. Keep chatting to her and maybe you'll learn more —like where her father is. He has a right to know about his daughter, don't you think?'

'Oh, I'd love her to find someone of her own, but then I'm on a similar mission and Oliver isn't sure it's right to hunt people down.'

'In most cases I'd go along with him on that, but in your case it's your duty to fulfil your mother's wish, and in Jenny's case she shouldn't be so alone in the world. She's an attractive girl, I can't believe no man is interested,' said Dave.

Veronica noticed the look of interest etched on Dave's face, but she quickly dismissed the notion as absurd. He found sophisticated women appealing— women of intelligence with beauty an added bonus, just as she found Oliver Linley intriguing, and not only for his good looks. She tried to heed the warning that too handsome a man can often lack depth, even sincerity,

but she was convinced that Oliver's integrity was un-
blemished. She was defending him even though she had
only known him for such a short time, but only a man of
genuine character would have come to her aid at
Kennedy in the way that he had done. The attraction
had been instant, but because she had thought he was a
face disappearing into the millions she had conditioned
herself to think as little as possible about him. Was it
the hand of fate which had led her to Brookville?
she wondered.

For a while she and Dave lazed over the breakfast
table, then she expressed her desire to take her shower.

'It'll be tea-time before we know it,' she said. 'And the
weather doesn't look too promising.'

'Storms are likely, so yes, we'd better get out if we're
to see the gardens in the dry,' he agreed.

Dave returned to his downstairs flat while Veronica
showered and dressed. She put on a pair of cotton slacks
with a matching top. It was still quite humid, but she
decided she had better take a lightweight jacket in case a
storm broke. An hour later she was sitting beside Dave
in his large fast car and they were speeding northwards,
laughing together over the pronunciation of Norwich
which didn't rhyme with 'porridge'!

When they reached Mohegan Park Veronica was
enchanted by the different varieties of roses in bloom in
the rose garden, especially the miniature ones. After
yesterday's storm the fragrance was particularly pun-
gent, and now that the sun had broken through between
the clouds the garden looked beautiful. Later they
bought grinders for lunch, huge bread rolls filled with
cold meats and salad which they took into the forest area
to enjoy. On the return journey they visited the shopping centre where the bank and post office were situated. Veronica pulled out the letter she had written to
the War Office, hesitated and put it out of sight again.
She wanted to know about her ancestors, yet she didn't
want to—or was it Oliver's influence which was making
her so indecisive? They shopped at the supermarket
before returning to Riverside, where Veronica invited

Dave up for tea. While she was preparing it she acted on impulse and gave him the letter to read.

'I'll have to rewrite it now, the date's wrong and it's beginning to look tatty,' she said. 'What shall I do, Dave? The years have passed. Will they care about a distant relative? Isn't it unfair to spring this surprise on them after all this time?'

Dave read the letter twice over and fingered it thoughtfully before replacing it in the envelope. 'The content of the letter is perfectly all right, Veronica,' he said. 'Whether you pursue it or not has to be your decision, but the longer you hesitate the less time you'll have to go visiting.'

'I know, that's what Natalie said. I wish I could pluck up courage and do it, but something's stopping me, I only wish I knew what it was.'

'Intuition? And sometimes hunches pay off. What do your sister and father think?'

'Ellie isn't really very concerned. She's probably longing for me to get home to take over the reins again, and Dad's of the opinion that it's best to let sleeping dogs lie, which doesn't help me very much. I came over here so full of enthusiasm, but now—I *must* do it, Dave, Mum wanted me to.'

'Then do it,' he advised.

Veronica felt that he wasn't very enamoured with the idea, so she put the letter on the kitchen worktop and tried to forget it, but it stared belligerently at her each time she went into the kitchen. The day had been pleasant enough, but it was as if they had run out of conversation, so at nine o'clock Dave stood up and said he would like to go and watch the baseball on television.

'You can watch it here if you like,' she invited.

Dave held her chin between his fingers, his smile not reflected in his eyes as he said lightly: 'I know you're being hospitable, but I doubt that baseball's quite your scene—besides, you've got that letter to rewrite.' He bent to kiss her good night as had become his custom, but Veronica found little pleasure in it tonight. She hated to be so cool, but her disappointment was back, and there was the prospect of tomorrow with nothing in particular to do.

The letter did not get rewritten. She paced the floor of her lounge, unable to settle after Dave had gone downstairs. She despised herself for her ineptitude, but suddenly she felt lonely, and with an empty ache of despondency which was quite uncharacteristic of her. She refused to admit that Oliver Linley had anything to do with it, yet she had been perfectly content before he had reappeared at Brookville.

She slept on next morning and after a combined breakfast and lunch she drove into Brookville to visit Jenny and Mrs Walcott, but before she reached the wards the lift paused at a midway floor and Oliver got in, accompanied by a petite woman wearing a red safari suit. She had bright chestnut-coloured hair styled in a french pleat, red button ear-rings on dainty ears, and her cheeks were gently tinged with a pink flush as she gazed up into Oliver's face. His blue eyes were laughing into the hazel-brown ones of the young woman who looked very young, hardly out of her twenties, Veronica assessed, and she cursed the stab at her own heart which reminded her of Dave's description of the type of women Oliver was reputed to prefer.

'Ah, Veronica, we were just going for a coffee. I'd like you to meet Maud Kishnev—Maud, this is Veronica Summers, from England.'

'A fellow countrywoman!' Maud exclaimed as she held out a warm hand in greeting. Now that Veronica was looking straight into her features she could see how wrong she had been about the woman's age, for, tiny though she was, there was a maturity of several years more than thirty. Veronica detected a foreign accent and decided that the name Kishnev could be Russian.

'How do you do,' she said hesitantly, glancing at Oliver, who was obviously impressed with Maud.

'Maud has come to perform brain surgery on a five-year-old boy,' he told her. 'He has a tumour, it's a delicate situation. There's no one better than Maud.'

'Brookville is one of Connecticut's best hospitals and I'm always delighted to be asked to come here to work,' said Maud. 'As Oliver says, this situation is tricky. The boy is an only child of parents in their forties. They never thought they'd have a child at all, and now this . . . It's very sad. I can only do the best I can, and with Oliver's support I hope we shall be able to remove the tumour completely.'

'When do you plan to operate?' asked Veronica.

'Tuesday, I think,' Oliver said. 'Maud must have time with the boy and his parents first, and she's only just arrived.' He turned to Maud Kishnev. 'I've been telling Veronica that she must try to see as much of America as possible during the year she's with us.'

Maud laughed. 'America is a very large country. There's so much to see, it's difficult to know where to start.'

'Have you lived here long?' Veronica queried politely.

Maud looked up at Oliver and something sensational passed between them as their memories entwined. Veronica felt the blush creep into her cheeks from embarrassment, but neither of them even glanced at her as their gaze remained locked in communication. It was minutes rather than seconds before Maud turned to Veronica. 'About ten years altogether,' she said softly, with an emotional crack in her voice. 'And Oliver has been such a wonderful friend to me during that time.'

'She's quite a wonderful person to befriend,' Oliver responded with mutual admiration.

In spite of her feelings Veronica accepted the offer to join them for coffee, if only to find out why Maud Kishnev was such a special person. Was this the woman she had visualised Oliver meeting down in Orlando? Maud wasn't quite what Veronica had expected. She was short rather than tall and sophisticated, and Veronica couldn't quite convince herself that the red outfit really complemented her colouring. Veronica could well remember her mother refusing to allow her to wear anything red because of the colour of her hair, yet it didn't look too awful on Maud, she decided. Maybe it was time she experimented a little more with her clothes. Wasn't Ellie always telling her she was too conservative, wearing what her younger sister described as drab unimaginative outfits. The conversation soon turned to the seriousness of the reason that Maud was at Brookville, which helped Veronica to feel more comfortable, and she quickly realised that Maud Kishnev was a most competent brain surgeon and dedicated doctor. She spoke with such deep affection for her patients that Veronica no longer felt the jealous pang that had gripped her when she first met Maud and Oliver together, but she didn't want to outstay her welcome, so she finished her coffee and stood up.

'Excuse me, but I'm on my way to visit Jenny,' she explained.

Oliver half rose from his chair, almost sat down, then stood up abruptly. 'But you're off duty, Veronica. I hope you weren't too angry with me for letting you down yesterday, but I wasn't sure which day Maud was coming.'

'It was all right, Oliver. Dave took good care of me.'

'But not today?'

'He had other plans, and this evening I shall meet up with Natalie and the others.'

'I don't want you to get into the habit of coming into Brookville on your days off.' There was an edge to his tone and Veronica felt herself stiffen at his rebuke. 'You need to refresh your mind and body during off-duty hours, Veronica.'

'I thought I was at liberty to spend my off-duty as I wish,' she replied stonily. 'Jenny needs some company, and I can spare an hour or so.' She wanted to tell him that she and Dave had discussed contacting Pinter's, but now was not the right time, so she nodded to Maud and left the cafeteria. All the way to the wards she felt her veins bubbling with irritation. Had Oliver tried to show her up in front of his lady friend, or was he genuinely concerned that she should get away from Brookville as much as possible? Her mood was not conducive to cheering up someone else, yet her feet took her decisively towards Jenny's room, where she found the younger girl sitting in an easy chair near the window.

'I thought I'd just look you up, Jenny,' Veronica greeted her with a smile. 'You could probably have found some company in the day room.'

Jenny's eyes cleared as she met Veronica's smile with a lift of her head. 'I've been in there all morning,' she said. 'And I've spent an hour with Mrs Walcott. For all her ninety odd years she's a fun lady, isn't she?'

'She has that reputation. She's quite a marvel. I suppose she's not sleeping quite so much now and I expect she appreciated your visit.'

'We got along well—but then I do seem to feel more comfortable with older women,' said Jenny. 'It's from being with my mother so much. I think I helped to cheer her up, and we had a laugh about Gloria and a few of the others. Hospitals are places where there are all sorts of secret relationships going on under cover.' Without giving Veronica the chance to comment about this Jenny hurried on: 'I've had a blood transfusion, and do you know, I can't remember when I felt so well! I'm still not sure whether I can trust the doctors here. They might be trying to boost my morale, but for the first time in ages I feel there's a glimmer of light at the end of the long dark tunnel.'

'That's really good news, Jenny,' Veronica said with genuine delight. 'And I can assure you that no one is simply trying to boost your morale. We know that with the right treatment you can be fit again, and that's what we're aiming for. It may take a little time, but once you've started to respond it'll accelerate and then there'll be no stopping you. I was wondering, Jenny —isn't there anyone from near where you live or from work who you'd like to visit you?' she added.

Jenny's expression changed at once. 'No,' she said adamantly. 'The neighbours aren't very interested, they weren't when Mum was alive, so they don't care about me. All they want is any snippets of gossip they can spread around.'

'Oh, Jenny, I'm sure that isn't true,' Veronica protested. 'Well, what about friends from work—even the place you worked at before you went to Pinter's?'

'No—I did have one or two nice girl friends there, but they all paired off with various boyfriends, and I wouldn't want Mark to know I was ill. I made the break, although I miss him dreadfully—yes, I'll admit it, I did care for him a great deal, but there's no future in that kind of relationship. I was brought up very strictly, in spite of Dad going off and leaving us, Mum taught me that marriage is a lasting contract for better or worse, so she'd never divorce Dad.'

'Jenny, don't you think you're being a bit hard on yourself? You and your father could start all over again now—after all, maybe there were things about your parents' marriage that you don't fully understand? Just as in this Mark's marriage—are you sure he isn't the innocent party?'

'There's no such thing as an innocent or a guilty party. If a marriage doesn't work they don't want it to work, they haven't tried to overcome their problems or talked it through properly.'

'So you don't blame your father entirely?'

Jenny's eyes flashed momentary anger, then with lips pursed she made a groaning sound in her throat. 'I had to stick by Mum and she blamed Dad, but no,' she sighed, 'I don't suppose he was any more to blame than her. Mum talked of him as being a rebel with a wandering eye, but she was rather undemonstrative, and I guess once I came along she had little time for him and his preferences. She taught me to hate him, but now that I'm on my own I find myself thinking about him a lot. I get mad at myself for it, because when all's said and done he did go away and never bothered about us.'

'Do you know where he is?' asked Veronica.

'I don't want to know. My attorney does, though, because there was the house to sign over to me after Mum died. It was jointly owned, you see, and for a while we didn't know whether my father would agree to the

way Mum wanted things done, but he agreed without any hesitation, which proves he didn't care what
happened to me.'

'Did he come to the funeral?'

'I specifically asked that he shouldn't, through the
attorney but . . . but I believe he was there. I'm afraid to
think that, but there was this man hanging around at the
cemetery among the trees. He was tall and looked so
sad, yet he had much too kind a face to be the man Mum
complained about.'

'Did you ever see any photos of him?' Veronica asked.

'Yes, but from way back when I was about five or six,
and of course he wouldn't look like that now. I'm
twenty-three, so he wouldn't recognise me either. It's
haunted me ever since, Veronica. Perhaps he did love
us, surely he must have done to come to the funeral, but
then I tell myself that it couldn't have been him after
all.'

'All this must have been so painful for you, Jenny.
When you feel stronger why don't you get in touch with
your attorney and ask to meet your father?'

'Oh, goodness me, no, I couldn't possibly do that,
Veronica! That would be like admitting Mum's guilt to
him.' Veronica insisted.

'I don't think he'd see it like that at all,' Veronica
insisted. 'He'd be overjoyed to see his daughter again.
It's worth thinking about, Jenny.'

'Oh, you!' Jenny said forcefully, 'full of bright ideas
which aren't practical. He's probably been living with
some other woman all these years and has a family of his
own. No, that would never work.'

But Veronica knew she had sown a seed of hope and
she planned to pursue the idea, though she'd have to talk
to Oliver and Dave about it first.

On her way home, though, she doubted that Oliver
would approve, and anyway, goodness knew when he
would be available to discuss such things. Maud Kishnev
was here to operate next Tuesday and she might well be
staying on after that to monitor her patient's progress.
Veronica would need to exercise patience, and she

didn't find this easy. When she wasn't in Oliver's company she found herself constantly warming to him. She tried to convince herself it was because he was English, because he had shown some consideration for her, but in her heart she was almost afraid to admit that she was in love with him. 'In love', though, was quite different from truly loving someone, and she told herself that she didn't know enough about Oliver Linley to really care for him, with allowances made for his indiscretions or peculiarities. She only knew what he was like on the surface, and he hardly knew her at all. With Maud it was so obviously different. They were very much aware of one another, in thought, word and deed, Veronica suspected. Theirs was an in-depth relationship, but where was it leading? And if they had known each other for so long why had it not come to fruition before this? She tortured herself with all sorts of imaginings. They were mature adults, both committed to their work, so maybe they grasped what happiness they could at infrequent intervals rather than embark on a part-time marriage. Veronica sat outside on the verandah in the late afternoon sunshine and wrote a letter to her father and Ellie, but after a rather poor attempt to explain away her lack of enthusiasm in trying to trace her grandfather she gave up. She had dozed in the relaxing chair when movement close by roused her sufficiently to open her eyes. Natalie was settling herself beside her with a tray of tea and cakes. She had moved a patio table between them, and now she smiled at Veronica as she poured some tea.

'Hope you don't mind being woken up. I've not been in long, so I decided to come out here and join you. Guess you never say no to a cup of tea?'

'I wonder what makes you think that!' Veronica scoffed lightheartedly. She raised herself up in the chair and moved the ratchet so that she was sitting in a higher position. 'I'm being terribly lazy,' she confessed. 'I tried to write to Dad and Ellie, but I'm not in the mood.'

'How's that? Too tired, or nothing to report?'

'Mm . . . nothing to report, not even any enthusiasm for trying to contact anyone. This wretched letter still sits in my bag. It needs rewriting, which is what I ought to be doing, but I just can't be bothered to do it. Dave read it and said it's OK, but I'm wary of getting involved with the authorities, I suppose.'

'Even if you send it off, Veronica, I believe you may draw a blank,' said Natalie. 'I've read somewhere that there are thousands of women in their forties who are now trying to trace their GI fathers, but the authorities here are reluctant to help them.'

'Lovely cuppa,' Veronica said appreciatively. 'Yes,' she sighed as she thoughtfully replaced her cup in the saucer, 'it's a dangerous project. I can understand why Mum wanted to know her father. It's strange that at some point in our lives we become intrigued by who we are and who our ancestors were. It's becoming quite the thing back home to make a family tree, but, when all's said and done, who does it benefit?'

'Just satisfies someone's curiosity, and it seems to me that having come this far you're afraid to delve any further. Like I told you, Veronica, the time slips by quite quickly, so don't leave it too late. The authorities, War Department or whoever can only say no—then where do you start looking?'

'I'd like to go to Rochester. My grandfather's father was a boat-builder, only on a small scale, I believe. They lived near a lake—Lake Eyrie, so at least I've got that to go on.'

'But that isn't much,' Natalie pointed out. 'It would be better to make some enquiries first.'

'It's knowing where to begin, Natalie, and I suppose Oliver put me off. He was quite sceptical about intruding into other people's lives, and in a way I agree with him. Yet, for Mum's sake—oh, I don't know—is it worth it?'

'I think it is,' Natalie said positively. 'You've come all this way and you'll hate yourself if you go home at the end of a year having achieved nothing. You have a name, I believe you said, so that should give you a lead. Write to the post office in Rochester and ask if they know of anyone by the name you've got.'

'It's a shot in the dark. There must be numerous

Duvalls about, and if I succeed in finding the right one he isn't going to be very pleased with me for turning up unexpectedly, and if I write first it could be embarrassing for him. I think it might be wiser to visit, at least I can make up some story about my grandmother knowing him during the war, after I've sussed out the situation. Of course, there's always the chance that he's dead anyway. From the little I know I reckon he'd be about seventy-two or three now.'

'Your grandmother's dead, I take it?'

'Yes, she died only two years before Mum. She must have loved Burt Duvall very much indeed, because she never married and devoted her life to looking after my mother. She was a sad person, looking much older than her sixty-three years when she died. She always lived with us; she and Mum were very close—strange that they died within a couple of years of each other. It wasn't until Mum was turning out some of her mother's things after she died that she found a couple of letters from another GI who we think must have been a friend of Burt Duvall's. They evidently went to France in June 1944. Mum was born in December of that year. She was already pretty ill by the time she found these letters, which is why she asked me to investigate. We don't even know if Burt Duvall made it after the D-Day landings.'

'Why did this friend write to your grandmother, then?' asked Natalie.

'That's what seems so strange to us. They're just ordinary friendly letters, though quite a lot of lines were blue-pencilled out, censored of course, probably because he'd mentioned locations, which wasn't permitted. But there was nothing in them to suggest that anything had happened to my grandfather, unless my grandmother had destroyed other letters before she died. For all we know there might have been correspondence between her and the American War Department. We suspect she'd forgotten about these two letters, but it only served to complicate things. If Mum hadn't found them she might not have got to

wondering about her father after such a long time. I want
to do what I can for her sake, but it'll be a thankless
task.'

'Your mother must have been very young when she
had you, then, if you say she was born at the end of
1944?'

Veronica laughed. 'Maybe it was because Mum wasn't
used to a man around the house. She'd met and married
my father by the time she was seventeen, and I was born
a year later. He was five years older than her, but by all
accounts Gran was equally besotted by this handsome
young man. Dad was good to both of them, I don't
remember any friction between them, which must be
quite rare when you've got your mother-in-law living in.
The only friction we've ever experienced has been with
Ellie. Maybe if I ever get to meet my grandfather I'll
understand why.' Veronica laughed, but said with an
affectionate note in her voice, 'She has to take after
someone, and we've never been able to fathom out
who.'

Natalie turned her head to listen to the distant screech
of brakes. 'Ah! Sounds to me as if our Dave has returned. You get to know the sounds of everyone coming
and going eventually. I wonder what he's been up
to—I'm surprised he didn't date you, Veronica, he's
pretty much intrigued, so watch your step.'

'I like Dave too, and we did go out together yesterday,
but I think he said he was visiting his parents today,'
Veronica told her.

'Mm . . . all the way down to New Haven, now I
wonder why he didn't take you along for the ride.'

'Oh no, why should he?' Veronica protested.

'He likes to show off his girlfriends.'

'Then evidently I'm not in the running.'

'Wouldn't you like to be?' Natalie asked in a whisper.

Before Veronica could answer Dave appeared around
the side of the house. As always he sounded cheerful and
made straight for the teapot. 'Can you spare a cup for a
dying man?'

'I never saw anyone less like dying,' Natalie quipped,

and leaned forward to pour out milk and tea into a spare cup which was on the tray.

'I wondered who the extra cups were for, now I know,' Veronica said, inclining her head in mock suspicion.

'I always bring an extra couple because someone's bound to arrive and it saves me getting up to fetch another one—or two—or three,' she laughed.

'So, girls, what's new?' asked Dave.

'Not a lot,' Natalie said as she squinted up at him against the glare of sunlight. 'And how was your trip? Veronica tells me you've been to see your folks.'

'That's right, but I might as well have saved myself the bother. They were just packing up for a trip to Washington. Dad has business there, so Mom's going along and they expect to be there for about a week. Still, I did my dutiful son act and drove them to the airport before driving back here. So, what say we all go out for a nice drive and drink somewhere?'

'Haven't you done enough driving for one day?' Natalie asked.

'Well, I didn't mean a long one—maybe just out to the Fort, take a walk along by the sea, have some refreshment before coming home.'

'I think you'd better count me out,' said Natalie, 'but you two go off and enjoy yourselves.'

'Now I could take that as a rebuff,' laughed Dave. 'I guess you're trying to be tactful, Natty, but I know Veronica would be quite happy for you to come along too. The change will do you good, and . . . er . . . your presence will prevent me from making a fool of myself where our delectable Veronica is concerned.' He raised his eyebrows quizzically as he glanced across at Veronica.

'Maybe she'd like you to make a fool of yourself.' Natalie suggested.

'I . . . I think her heart may be elsewhere, and anyway she's bent on trying to trace her unknown family. No time for idle ne'er-do-wells like me.' His boyish face was wreathed in smiles.

'You know you're only fishing for compliments, Dave

Wilfroy,' Veronica put in. 'Actually I do want to talk to you about Jenny Pearson. I went in to see her today, and she talked a little about her father. I'm sure deep down she'd like to meet him.'

'Right, then let's make this a strictly "help Jenny" trip, and you can come as chief adviser, Natty. I'll go and freshen up and meet you both here in half an hour.' Dave drained his cup and went into the house.

'I don't have to come, Veronica,' Natalie said seriously.

'There's nothing between us,' Veronica said. Was there just the hint of disappointment in her voice? 'We like each other very much. Dave's good company, but it's no use me getting involved in serious relationships when I shall be returning to England when my year is up.'

'Marriage would be a reason for staying?' Natalie intimated.

'Heavens, I've only been here a few weeks yet!' Then she looked at Natalie with a sombre expression. 'Please come. I really do want to help Jenny. Maybe it's because we have something in common, losing our mothers through similar illness, but I'm lucky in that I have my father and the incorrigible Ellie. It must be terrible to be so alone in the world. Jenny is an intelligent girl, but she needs some enjoyment in her life. Having been hurt by this married man friend she's lost her sense of fun, and her ability to trust men in general, but somewhere there must be a man just right for her, and I feel certain her father would be over the moon to get together with her. She told me she's sure he was at her mother's funeral. She could well have got things wrong about her parents —after all, she's never heard her father's side of things.'

'I have to admit to being less than patient with her over this business of anticipating fatal illness. I do realise, though, that it's being so alone which has brought on the depression, and I agree that we should be doing all we can to help her—on the other hand, Veronica, there are special counselling departments for people like her which I expect Oliver will refer her to when he's done all the investigating he needs to do.'

Veronica stood up and began to pack up the crockery on the tray. She knew Natalie was politely telling her that she might be getting too involved with Jenny, but the girl needed a friend. In some ways she reminded Veronica of Ellie, whose hang-ups and sometimes strange behaviour could be attributed to the fact of losing her mother when in her teens.

'We all react differently to the punches life throws at us,' she said philosophically. 'Some of us can take them, some appear not to be emotionally disturbed at the time, but after a few months, years even, the victim can crack up. We all need a friend at some time in our lives.'

'True enough,' Natalie agreed, pulling herself out of the relaxer chair and following Veronica into the house. 'I'll take Dave up on the offer of a drive out to the Fort. It'll make a nice change not to have to drive myself, and to have a bit of company.'

'Then we'll try not to talk too much shop!'

The trip was a pleasant one, the evening air balmy as Dave drove slowly along the coast road out to the Fort, and afterwards they stopped on the homeward route for sandwiches and coffee. Veronica expounded all that she had learned from Jenny Pearson during their afternoon chat, and Dave seemed genuinely interested in helping her.

'We must take things gradually,' he said, 'But I think a call to Pinter's might open up some new avenues for Jenny. I did manage to see my parents long enough to ask them if they knew anything about the firm, and Dad assured me that they're renowned for being good to their staff. I'm sure they must have a personnel officer or social worker on the staff, and I'm rather surprised that no one has made enquiries about Jenny. Then again, she may have refused any kind of attention, so we don't want to upset the applecart. I'll have a word with Oliver as soon as I can.'

But the days passed, and all Oliver was concerned with was Maud Kishnev and her young patient, who after several days of being in intensive care began to make good progress.

Oliver did an occasional morning round at a speed which was not particularly satisfying to his patients, but they didn't seem to mind being in Dave's capable hands.

'I'm going to give Pinter's a ring,' Dave said one morning as they went through some of their patients' records. 'I'm not sure what Oliver's reaction will be, but Jenny has made real strides over this past week and should be ready for discharge shortly. She's got quite a sparkle in her eyes now, so I feel that some effort should be made to liaise with the people she works for. She'll need keeping an eye on after she leaves here, and there's not much we can do if she goes down to New Haven.'

Veronica left Dave's office to help Mrs Walcott get bathed and dressed, and later she went along to Jenny's room. She found her standing on the bed trying to see herself in the only small mirror in the room which was on the inside of the wardrobe door.

'What on earth——?' Veronica began, then both girls laughed.

'I'm trying to decide what to wear,' said Jenny. 'You never know, this might be my lucky day and Dr Linley will come to see me. I must remember to complain as I feel thoroughly neglected. Now, what do you think, Veronica, the blue silk, or the red cotton?'

'I think you must get down from there before you fall. Personally I like the blue, but silk is a bit dressy for this occasion, so go for the red, but put some make-up on. Evidently you've had your hair done, it looks so silky this morning, Jenny.'

Veronica knew that this was a good sign that Jenny was taking some trouble with her appearance, and she hoped Oliver would begin to take an interest in his patients again soon. How soon was sooner than she had anticipated. While she watched Jenny experimenting with lipstick, blusher and nail varnish, heavy footsteps could be heard farther along down the passage and then quite loud voices preceded the entrance of Oliver, followed by Dave and Gloria.

Oliver had his head bent as he pored over the notes in his hand, and when at last he looked up it was evident that he was surprised.

'Mm . . .' he mumbled, 'quite a transformation, I see, Jenny.'

'For the better, I hope, Dr Linley?'

'Certainly that,' he agreed. 'Your blood is in good shape and all the tests we did proved negative, so in a few days, if you maintain this kind of progress, I expect you'd like to get out of here?'

Jenny's face clouded momentarily, then she brightened. 'It won't be easy to go back to work. I shall feel like a new girl again, but I've got to start somewhere now that I know I'm not for the scrap heap.'

'I wasn't suggesting work just yet, my dear,' Oliver said, obviously impressed with Jenny's determination to return to normal. 'Why not a holiday first? Have you any relatives you could stay with, or a friend perhaps?'

Jenny looked embarrassed as she shook her head. 'There's no one, but I really don't mind going home if I can get back to work. I feel as if my brain has seized up and is bursting to be let free again.'

'That's an excellent indication that you're returning to normal health, Jenny, but I don't think it's a good idea to go straight from hospital to work without some intermediary time to get readjusted. A few more days and we'll consider how we can overcome that problem.' He turned suddenly to look intently at Veronica. 'I'm sure you can come up with some useful suggestions, Veronica?'

Veronica was rather surprised that he should consult her on the subject, or had Dave already revealed to Oliver their concern over Jenny?

'I'm sure a holiday is a splendid idea,' she agreed. 'Don't you have special facilities for someone like Jenny who has no family?'

'Mm . . . well, yes, but mostly it's middle-aged to elderly who need such accommodation, like Mrs Walcott for instance.' He paused, stroking his chin thoughtfully before committing himself. 'I wonder,' he said slowly. 'Mrs Walcott is about ready for a rest home for a few weeks, how would you like to go along for company, Jenny?'

'Now it does sound as if you're putting me out to grass with the senior citizens!' she laughed.

'No way am I suggesting that you're going to be looked after—it'll be the other way around, my dear. I'm thinking of a lovely country house divided up into units, managed by a retired nurse who only has volunteers to help with the running of the house. It's not so much that you need convalescence as company, and something positive to do to prepare you for a busy work schedule. There's no rush to make a decision, but think about it, Jenny.' Oliver closed her folder and led the way to see his next patient.

Jenny met Veronica's uncertain stare, then burst into laughter. 'He's a case, isn't he? Here am I, a computer programmer, aged twenty-three, and he's suggesting that I go into an old people's home!'

'That's not quite true, Jenny,' Veronica corrected. 'They won't all be as old as Mrs Walcott, but it isn't such a bad idea, you know. For one thing, Mrs Walcott will be very glad of your company.'

'I'd still rather go home, I think. Suddenly I feel I want to be preparing my own meals, doing my laundry, and wondering what mail there might be waiting for me.'

'Haven't you been in touch with *anyone* since you came into hospital?'

'Only my attorney. He has a key and he promised he'd go round to my house and check that things were OK. He was going away on holiday, though, so I haven't heard from him lately.'

'How much does your employer know about your illness?'

'Oh, I've kept them informed of where I am. Big concerns don't care what's happening to you if you can't work. They're only interested in when I'm going back.'

'I'm sure they care more than you think, Jenny, and they'll be delighted to hear that you're better. A holiday first, though, is a must. You could go on a package

tour somewhere nice—Bermuda, or the Bahamas?'
Veronica laughed, but Jenny was thoughtful.

'Yes,' she answered slowly, 'I could, but I'm not ready
to face a lot of strangers. That's why I'm not in favour of
Dr Linley's idea, still, I like old Mrs Walcott and I'd feel
I was doing her a favour.'

'You don't have to make up your mind yet, but it's
certainly worth considering.'

It seemed, though, that Jenny didn't need to think it
over for long, as a week later she was packing up to leave
Brookville, and Veronica was delighted to be helping
Mrs Walcott to do the same.

'I must confess I never thought this day would come,'
the old lady said in her husky voice. 'I'd rather be going
home, but I'm thrilled to bits that young Jenny is coming
with me. She's a nice kid and I feel sorry for her. It's
tough being left alone in the world, but her time here has
been well spent. She thinks the world of you, Veronica,
and Dr Linley, of course, not to mention that nice Dave
Wilfroy—but I fancy she's got this notion that you and
he are—well, you know . . .'

'You can set her mind at rest about that, Mrs Walcott.
Dave and I are good friends, and there was a time when
even I thought we could become something more, but
we've settled to be just good pals.'

Mrs Walcott raised her frail eyes to peer into Veronica's face with a decidedly wicked twinkle, but she
only mumbled in reply, and Veronica wondered what
that was supposed to mean!

CHAPTER FIVE

AT HER mid-morning break a few days later Dave joined Veronica for coffee.

'So, how does it feel to be back on Outpatients again? he enquired.

'I miss my two special patients, it was nice to have time to get to know Mrs Walcott and Jenny, and they've promised to keep in touch.'

Dave leaned across the table with obvious intrigue. 'I thought you'd like to know that with Oliver's permission I telephoned Pinter's,' he told her.

'Oh? Oliver agreed to it?' she asked in surprise.

'He's not that unfeeling towards his patients, Veronica, and he was pleased to think we cared enough about Jenny to want to help her any way we could. I spoke to the personnel officer, who was quite forthcoming. She said Jenny seemed reluctant to talk about herself or become involved in social events connected with the firm. She had her own ideas as to why Jenny was so introverted and they were planning to try to bring her out, but they also realised that she was far from well. Now, the two guys who work with her are going to make a trip up to see her at the weekend and hope to establish some kind of social relationship. One of them is married, so they're all coming, wife and kids too, isn't that great?'

'Excellent, I'm so pleased, but . . .'

'But what?' Dave's happy expression faded.

'I wish we could find her father. If only we knew who her attorney is, I'm sure he'd be as pleased as us to put them in touch again.'

'Now hold on, Veronica. Don't let's get carried away —that, Oliver definitely would not like,' Dave warned adamantly. 'I agree it's a lovely idea and I'd have no difficulty in finding out who her attorney is, because I believe she put him down as her next of kin, which we thought was rather odd at the time. I've no doubt that if he's in contact with her father then he's keeping him informed of Jenny's welfare, and we must leave things to work themselves out naturally.'

'There's nothing natural in having a father and not speaking to him through no fault of your own,' she protested, 'and I'm sure Jenny's mother couldn't have been thinking rationally not to allow him to see Jenny.'

'I know you're right and I'd love to do more to help Jenny, but we must take things slowly. She has to go back to work of necessity to earn her living, so that has to be top priority, and if these guys visit her it'll make her feel wanted at least.'

'I should think she could be quite a popular girl. She seems to enjoy her work, it's just getting her out of her shell.'

'Work colleagues are just the people to do that, and now that they know a little bit of her background maybe they'll be able to get through to her.' Dave sighed. 'I wouldn't mind being able to get through to her myself.'

'You're really keen?' asked Veronica.

'I find her attractive, though what she's like away from the hospital is another thing.'

Veronica smiled and gave him a nudge. 'There's only one way to find out, Dave. Ask her for a date,' she urged.

'Not advisable when she's still a patient of ours, but maybe when she's discharged completely I will.' He drank the rest of his coffee in total silence and Veronica guessed he was quite disappointed that Jenny had left Brookville. She knew he often went along to see her when he was off duty if only for a few minutes, but it proved that his interest was more than doctor-patient, and Veronica thought they would make a good combination. She wished her own life could be sorted out so easily. She had no feeling of malice towards Jenny for capturing Dave's heart, on the contrary, she was glad for both of them, but the man who occupied so much of her daydreams was elusive. She saw him only briefly while Maud was around, and the petite doctor didn't seem in any hurry to return to Orlando. Veronica had noticed them leaving Brookville together on a couple of occasions and whenever she bumped into Oliver, Maud was never far behind.

'Do you know how long Dr Kishnev is staying at Brookville?' she asked suddenly.

Dave came out of his reverie and stared at her, his expression brightening with humour at her question. 'She isn't staying here,' he said confidently. 'She always stays with Oliver at his bungalow.'

'I didn't know he had a bungalow.'

'Oh yes, our esteemed director needs a hideaway. He only uses the flat here for convenience. The bungalow is in a lovely rural setting at East Lyme.'

Veronica felt her spirits sag. She knew she was being foolish, after all, Oliver's admiration for Maud Kishnev was hardly a secret, and yet she tortured herself with hope. Hope that one day she might see this bachelor bungalow, that soon Maud would go back to where she belonged, and yet knowing that if there was a strong bond between them which had lasted for several years it was hardly likely to be broken now—and yet, she argued mentally, if it hadn't led to marriage after all this time then surely it wasn't on the cards in the foreseeable future. Commonsense told her, though, that with their respective demanding careers they might have opted for the kind of life they appeared to enjoy. Suddenly she felt Dave's hand on her back. 'Cheer up, Veronica! You're going to be far too busy chasing your ancestors for romantic interludes.' He stood up, hesitated as if there was something he wanted to add, then thought better of it and walked away, leaving Veronica alone with her sense of dismal failure. She must do something about Rochester, and her grandfather, Burt Duvall. Wasn't that the reason she was here? Not to embark on entanglements of the heart, she reasserted.

The days passed and Veronica was much too busy to think of going to Rochester. With the long hot days of summer came the innumerable accidents on the road

and on the sea. Outpatients' clinics were heavy, the
wards full and the staff's off-duty filled with beach
parties and barbecues, which Veronica frequently
attended. She had gone off duty one evening with every
intention of going to Bluff Point with the usual crowd,
but when she reached Riverside there was a letter
awaiting her. She felt a pang of guilt when she saw that it
was from Ellie, and her brain buzzed with all manner of
excuses she intended to relate to her sister for not
carrying out the search for their grandfather. She made
straight for the bedroom and began undressing, while in
between she opened Ellie's letter. It wasn't the usual
air-letter, she noticed, but a thicker package in a long
white envelope. Ellie was not the best of scholars and
certainly not fond of putting pen to paper, so Veronica
was suspicious. Perhaps her father had decided to write,
probably to enquire why her letters were sparse and
somewhat vague, scolding her for not getting on with the
proposed task. She was down to her bra and pants, her
mind ahead to the hour or two she anticipated spending
by the sea, when she stopped in her tracks. With trem-
bling fingers she unfolded a single sheet of notepaper,
allowing another letter to fall to the bed. She sat down
heavily beside it, half afraid to open and read the
contents. Ellie was full of excitement, but Veronica
was overcome with apprehension at the old letter to
her grandmother from Burt Duvall which Ellie had
enclosed.

'Dad thought he'd like to get the attic turned out while
you're away,' Ellie wrote. 'It was fun. I never dreamed
Mum had kept so many of our old toys, books and
games, but the biggest surprise was when we uncovered
an old suitcase which it seems belonged to Gran. She'd
kept all Burt Duvall's letters tied up with red ribbon, but
this one seems the most significant, as it was written a
long time after the war.'

Veronica read the first half, but could read no more
because of the tears which ran down her cheeks . . .

*   *   *

She was late arriving at Bluff Point. It had taken her a
long while to get over the shock of discovering that Burt
Duvall had kept up a correspondence with her grandmother and begged her to go out to America after the
war, but Betty Smith had refused, and finally after an
apparent silence of several years he wrote saying that he
had reluctantly given up waiting and had married someone else.

Veronica had needed a hot bath to steam her complexion and restore it to its usual texture with all signs of
weeping abated. Now she parked her car and was locking it up when a deep voice intruded into her troubled
thoughts. 'Dare I hope you're looking particularly
peeved because I've neglected you of late, Veronica?'

She felt his presence, had done a moment before he
spoke, and she wished with all her heart that Oliver
Linley had not sought her out just at this moment.

'Peeved isn't quite the right word, Oliver,' she said,
trying to hide the pain in her voice.

'My darling!' he exclaimed with concern, clutching
her arm and turning her round to face him. 'Whatever's
the matter?'

Veronica took one swift glance into his eyes, was
instantly absorbed by his anxious expression and dissolved into a new tide of emotion. Oliver led her away
from the noise of the crowd, none of whom had ever
noticed that Veronica had arrived. He cradled her head
against his chest and allowed her to weep, while in
faltering words she explained the contents of her grandfather's letter of so long ago.

'You're an old romantic, sweet Veronica,' he crooned
in a humorous tone.

'It's not funny,' she snapped angrily, wishing she had
stayed at Riverside. 'Just think of all the years they
wasted, and my poor mother never knowing her father.
It's all so unfair!'

'Ah,' Oliver replied solemnly. 'Life is seldom fair. It
wasn't your grandfather's fault if he wanted your grandmother to come to America. She couldn't expect him to
wait for ever, now could she?'

Veronica didn't answer. She knew he was right, but all she could think of was the desperate plea her mother had made for her to try to find Burt Duvall. Now she had a different address, still in Rochester, but she felt unprepared for the task ahead.

'I shall have to go to Rochester now,' she said.

'Don't be in too much of a rush, Veronica. Sleep on it for a few nights. Think of the shock you're going to give your grandfather—that's if he's still alive.'

'But that's what I must find out,' she cried.

'You could write first. Forgive me if you think I'm interfering, but wouldn't that be the most sensible thing to do?'

'Sensible! None of this is sensible,' Veronica exploded. 'I'm sorry, I shouldn't be bothering you with my problems.'

'Everyone's problems at Brookville are mine too, Veronica,' said Oliver. 'I'm sorry I haven't been available recently to talk about old Mrs Walcott and Jenny Pearson, but I don't see Maud that often, and when she makes one of her rare visits to Groton I have to confess I like to keep her here for as long as I can.' He gave a deep sigh as if he too might have problems of his own, and Veronica wished she hadn't confided in him, but he slid his arm around her waist and guided her along the shore of the point and then among the trees. 'You say that your grandfather kept up correspondence with your grandmother for quite some time before he finally decided he couldn't wait any longer? I wonder why she was so reluctant to come to America? Most people would have jumped at the chance.'

'She had my mother to bring up alone,' she explained. 'Maybe she couldn't face the travelling with a child of six, which my mother must have been when this letter was written in 1950. She must have had good reason, I'm sure, but she certainly broke Burt Duvall's heart. He wrote such lovely letters, he must be a wonderful man, and that's what makes me so sad. Ellie has found a stack of letters, but she could only send this one. Even she is quite overcome by what she's found, and that's saying something for Ellie.'

'He'll have a new family now, my dear Veronica, and you must be prepared for rejection.' Veronica stiffened and tried to disengage herself from Oliver's grasp, but he held on firmly. 'I know that displeases you, but it's only right you should be warned. I can't bear to see you so upset, Veronica.' His voice changed from its usual abrupt decisiveness to tender understanding, and Veronica went limp in his embrace. The moment his lips touched hers she felt as if she were floating in a warm lagoon of safety, and she needed no encouragement to meet his persuasive demands. He cleverly cast his spell; crowd noises blended and faded with the evening light as dusk settled over them like a soft mantle, excluding them from the party.

'I can quite understand your grandfather's persistence if you take after your grandmother,' Oliver whispered. 'But I doubt that I could exercise such patience. Had I been in his shoes I'd have had to catch the next ship or plane to go after the woman I loved.'

Veronica drew back. Was this just a metaphorical comparison on his part, or was he trying to indicate how much he loved Maud? And if he loved Maud so much then how could he dally with her so eagerly? His way of consoling her, she supposed, and she knew she should have stopped him but it was too much like a dream come true.

'As far as we can tell Burt Duvall was never told that Betty Smith had a child by him,' she said. 'The only reason my mother could think of was that her mother didn't want him to marry her simply because he'd given her a baby.'

'But there has to be a reason for her keeping such a thing from him. I realise that you feel you want to know just as your mother did, but would your grandmother agree to this enquiry after all these years—over forty, in fact?'

Veronica fell silent, content to remain close to this elegant man whose influence was so important to her. His hand slid down her bare arm until her fingers were locked in his. She looked up into his blue eyes and responded to his telling smile with an expression of satisfaction. Oliver drew her hard against his chest until she could feel the pounding of his heart beating a rhythm in tune to her own. When his mouth came down hard on hers she opened her lips greedily, and her head spun like a top. But the top ran out of steam and Oliver's passion stabilised as he swung her round and proceeded to walk among the tall trees in the centre of the peninsula with the sea gently lapping on either side.

'I can only repeat that my advice is for you to write first to the address you have in Rochester,' he suggested. 'Then according to the reply you get you can arrange further enquiries around that.'

'Yes, that would be the best thing to do. I don't want to put my foot in it, or make trouble for his family, and it might save a useless trip.'

Veronica noticed that they were walking away from the rest of the party, where the point was widening and in consequence the wooded area more dense. Suddenly she looked up and noticed that everywhere little lights were darting in the warm evening air. Oliver was aware of what she saw, and his chuckle was intimately seductive.

'Fireflies,' he explained. 'Romantic beetles if you like, but not seen at home. The nearest thing England has is the glowworm.'

'Don't they look pretty flitting about among the trees? No wonder they feature in love-songs.'

'Of course, they glow to attract a mate, and they're particularly busy on the wing at night.' She felt the pressure of his touch intensify at her waist and knew he was feeling romance in the air, just as she did. But it was only lighthearted romance, she reminded herself. Oliver was committed first to his work and secondly to his beloved Maud. He was only showing dutiful concern for her in her dilemma and because he felt responsible being that she was so far from home.

'Shouldn't we be getting back to the party?' she dared to suggest.

'Afraid of the dark?' he said wickedly. 'Surely not with all these fireflies to bewitch you?'

'I don't know about being bewitched,' she laughed, 'I do know I'm hungry!'

Oliver tut-tutted in mock disappointment, and they strolled back towards the picnic spot where the barbecue was in full swing. Veronica doubted that they had been missed, but now that she had talked with Oliver she felt able to forget about going in search of her grandfather for a short while, and was happy to enjoy the party.

There were sausages and hamburgers with fried onion, a generous supply of fresh rolls, and the popping of corks could be heard constantly, but Veronica was abstemious until she had eaten well. One or two of the male staff had their boats moored nearby and people began to pair off and disappear. Veronica watched with interest as she sat on a tree stump and sipped her white wine. The frolic began and some of the girls were thrown into the water, but Veronica decided it was time to leave. Instantly Oliver was beside her.

'Had enough?' he asked gently.

'It's been lovely to be out in the fresh air, but now I'm ready to go home. Thanks for listening to my tale of woe, Oliver. I know I'm silly to be so emotional about it all, but I'm just so sorry that Mother didn't find out more about the truth while she was alive.' She stood up and began to walk towards her car with Oliver at her side. 'Maybe Gran thought that after she had died Mum would have found the letters, but Mum was never well enough to get up in the attic sorting out old belongings.'

'And your father?'

'He was always so wrapped up in business until Mum was found to be suffering from an incurable disease, then he devoted his time to her welfare. The past gets forgotten in those circumstances, yet Mum must have been lying there day after day torturing herself with the desire to know more about her father. I only wish——'

Oliver placed his fingers over her lips. 'Useless to wish for the impossible, my dear. Wherever your mother is I'm sure she knows you did your best and will continue to do so.' He smiled reassuringly as he took his fingers away. 'Um—you have your own car,' he said, giving the matter undue attention. 'Follow me back to Brookville, then a nice cup of coffee or tea before we retire?'

Veronica's spirits lifted and she agreed readily. After the ten-minute drive back to the hospital Oliver guided her to a side entrance which opened into a small square lobby where he summoned a lift.

She knew that most things in the States were large and luxurious, but she wasn't quite prepared for the space and modern décor of Oliver's penthouse apartment. Everywhere was tastefully decorated and furnished, the lounge with large, soft leatherette chairs and sofas, and the kitchen made her gasp with amazement at the gadgets installed there. She was speechless with admiration. 'It's all so . . . so . . .' she gasped.

Oliver laughed. 'I know exactly what you mean, Veronica. A little too much so for my tastes. I prefer a nice log fire and a little colour to give a warm friendly atmosphere, but this goes with the job, so I'm not complaining.' He switched the kettle on and opened the tea-bag jar. 'I know I can count on you to enjoy a cup of tea, rather than the usual coffee. With Maud here for several days I've had my fill of coffee!'

Veronica noticed he didn't mention his bungalow, and she didn't enlighten him that she knew where Maud usually stayed. She assumed Maud had left to return to Orlando, but she refrained from asking.

'Everything here is for convenience,' he explained, passing the tea-tray through the serving hatch from the ultra-clean-looking grey and white kitchen to the lounge. 'The micro-wave for fast cooking, the dishwasher means I don't have to don an apron too often —of course, it's all looked after by domestic staff, who do rather pamper me. It suits me well enough for weekday working, then I can take myself off to my own bungalow for weekends if I'm lucky. You must come to visit me there some time, Veronica,' he added. 'It's away from Brookville, set in rural surroundings which remind me of England, and I think you'll like it.'

'It sounds very nice,' she said politely. 'I'd love to see it.' She went to the big picture lounge window which overlooked the grounds of Brookville and beyond towards the river. 'We're very high up,' she observed. 'How many storeys high?'

'Not so many really, six actually, but Brookville itself is built on high ground so is above the normal street level to start with. I agree that up here is quite divorced from the hospital, yet I can be on the wards or in theatre in minutes when required. Dave is on call this evening, though, so I'm free. You seem to get along with him very well?'

So that was it! Suddenly Veronica realised why she had been asked up for refreshment when it would have been much simpler to go straight home to bed. He wanted to know about her and Dave.

'I suppose Dave was the first person I worked with, so I got to know him much quicker than anyone else. He's nice, and so friendly, you can't help but like him.'

'Quite the heart-throb where women are concerned, though I'm sure he's the sort who will eventually marry and settle down. Yes, Dave is quite a character,' Oliver added pointedly.

'He's good at his job,' Veronica defended. 'Ambitious without being a bore.'

'Mm . . . do you think I'm a bore, Veronica?' He held back the cup of tea he had just poured and was passing to her, and his eyes twinkled down at her mischievously.

She inclined her head, pursed her lips thoughtfully and replied equally impishly: 'Can I refrain from answering that on the grounds that it might incriminate me?'

Oliver raised his dark satin-smooth eyebrows and let her take the tea. 'Evidently I am,' he said with a hint of remorse. 'But I'm afraid the medical profession here is rather like big business at home, and you only get on if you're ambitious.'

'There's nothing wrong with being ambitious, especially when it's combined with a genuine desire to be of service to the community and to help others. What made you choose America in the first place, Oliver?'

He looked directly into her eyes, but he wasn't seeing her, she realised. Then, digging his hands into his trouser pockets, he walked over to the window. There was a strained silence and Veronica wished she hadn't asked such a personal question, so she said hurriedly: 'I'm sorry, I wasn't prying—it was just——'

'Polite conversation? Idle curiosity?' he tossed over his shoulder.

'Certainly not that,' she snapped irritably. 'There are many reasons why a doctor decides to practise in another country.'

Another more prolonged silence, then: 'I could say for love of a good woman. Misplaced love, misguided love—I know that now—you see, Veronica, Maud and I worked together some years ago. I admired her talent so much that I mistook my esteem for something much deeper, sadly to the point of embarrassing her. I was a young housemen at the time in London, she was already a consultant. I didn't realise I was making myself a nuisance, and that wasn't my intention, I simply adored her, so she came to New York.' He swung round and faced Veronica. 'Why the hell am I explaining this to you?—it's something I never talk about.'

Veronica stood up, her face tight with confusion. 'I shouldn't have come here, I'll leave immediately.'

'Sit down. I want to tell you, I must, and I'm glad you asked why I came here.' Oliver withdrew his hands from his pockets and dragged them down his face, leaving the traces of a very tired man exposed. 'I was a foolish young man, and I'm ashamed to say it took an older, wiser doctor to tell me why Maud had left London. I had to leave that hospital as soon as I'd finished the course I was on. I felt so . . . so . . . stupid!' He bit the word out as if he hated himself. 'After a suitable time I knew I had to find Maud, convince myself that I wasn't in love with her—well, of course I was *in* love with her, but not the kind of love marriages require—and apologise to her for the damage I'd done. So you see, Veronica, I know what it's like to search, trace, and try to appease the past.'

'It sounds to me as if you're blaming yourself need-lessly,' Veronica said softly.

Oliver laughed suddenly in his deep, throaty way as he sat down beside her on the sofa. 'I've blamed myself persistently. The UK could have done with Maud's knowledge and expertise.'

'She didn't have to run away, though, did she? She could have told you your feelings were misplaced?'

'She didn't want to hurt me,' he explained.

'Then she must have had some finer feelings for you—perhaps more than she cared to admit.'

Oliver thought this over, then his expression clouded briefly before it lightened again. 'You could be right. Every time we meet something chemical clicks between us.'

'I know, I could tell,' Veronica dared to confess.

'Is it *that* obvious? No, I can't believe that, someone must have told you, but who? No one knows—that is, only Gloria.'

'No one has mentioned anything to me about you and Maud, honestly. But the day I met you together in the lift and you introduced me I just felt that there was—' she shrugged, 'something. I promise I won't breathe a word to anyone, after all it's none of my business. She's a very charming person.'

'Much more than that, Veronica, but you don't know her as I do. And for the record, I'm over my hang-up about her in that way. I'll always admire her more than any other doctor I know, I shall always treasure her as one does a very special person, we understand each other and we shall continue to care about each other, but her work is her life.'

Veronica wanted to tell him she understood that his devotion to his profession matched that of Maud, but she wanted to hope it didn't entirely. That somewhere deep inside this extraordinary man was a tiny space for a woman to give her all to him, and the more she was with him the more she loved him. It was useless to deny.

'That's very commendable,' she said now, 'but everyone has to make room for human relationships and personal happiness.'

He reached across and grasped her hand in his. 'That's a nice thing to say, Veronica. We're all searching for happiness; whether we find it or not is usually up to us.'

'Sometimes other people lead us along a wrong track. Take Jenny Pearson, for instance,' she said, 'I suppose her mother thought she was making a happy life for her daughter, but now that she's gone what has Jenny got? A lonely existence, a frightening one even, when maybe she could be reunited with her father, who would be her friend and protector.'

'Ah! I wondered when you would get around to that subject. Dave told me that you and he had been conspiring together to interfere in a patient's private life.'

'How can you think that?' she protested. 'I'm sorry for Jenny. I've got to know her pretty well since you assigned me to look after her and I'm over the moon to see the change in her, but I still feel her mother was wrong to deprive her ex-husband of seeing their daughter. It's made Jenny grow up despising him, and yet she's never given him a chance.'

'Just as your grandmother evidently never gave your grandfather a chance,' Oliver countered.

'That's why I'm here, to try to put a wrong right.'

'And maybe bring distress to the lives of a whole family? It's important to know when, and when not, to interfere, Veronica.'

'My interference, as you call it, could bring a great deal of joy to my grandfather and his family. If he isn't dead then perhaps he'll be pleased to know all about the women he loved, and their child. And as for Jenny, if she doesn't make friends easily then it will be good if her workmates visit and cheer her up, make her feel that she's been missed and is liked. Sometimes, Oliver, we need a little helping hand in the right direction, call it interference if you must, but few of us can do without it at some time in our lives.'

'I can't sanction any helping hand where Jenny and

her father are concerned, and if you and Dave go behind my back I shall be extremely angry. Meeting up with him when she doesn't even know what kind of man he is could create more problems for her, and I have to consider her welfare as my patient. What you do about your own family is your affair.'

'I'd like to save up some days off so that I can go to Rochester,' Veronica said positively. 'Oh, I'll write to the address Ellie has sent, but if I hang around I shall never make any progress.'

Oliver stood up abruptly, and she knew he didn't approve, which made her all the more determined.

Now he was dismissing her, and she felt as she walked away from the side entrance that she had lost all hope of ever getting to know him better. He went with her to her car. 'I'll follow you to Riverside,' he said, as she slid into the driver's seat.

Veronica laughed scornfully. 'Good heavens,' she said, 'I wouldn't dream of letting you do that. I'm quite capable of driving myself home, thank you.' Oliver slammed the door and stood aside as she backed out of the space where she had parked, but as she drove along the main road towards the river she knew that the car travelling at a suitable distance behind her was Oliver making sure she reached Riverside safely. She kept her eye on him in the mirror and smiled to herself when she indicated that she was to turn off, but he kept right there with her, yet when she pulled up in the ground of Riverside there was no sign of him.

The house was in darkness, after all it was well past midnight, and although she prepared for bed she knew she had too much on her mind to go to sleep, so she curled up on the bed, and after re-reading Ellie's letter and the old one from her grandfather to her grandmother she began composing her own letter to him. She simply said that Betty Smith was her grandmother and that old letters from him had been discovered, and as she was working in Groton she thought she might like to take a trip across New York State to Rochester. She didn't need to rewrite it as she was satisfied with her first

attempt, so she stamped it ready to post in the morning.
But still sleep wouldn't come, as now her thoughts went
over all that she and Oliver had said.

She couldn't help wondering why he had confided in
her his feelings for Maud simply in answer to her question about why he had come to America to work. What
he felt for Maud was infinitely more than a close working
relationship, and Veronica still held the picture in her
mind's eye of Maud's admiration for Oliver. But if he did
feel strongly about Maud surely he wouldn't have
reacted to her the way he had? She would always cherish
the feel of his smooth velvety lips on her own, and God,
what a mess she must have looked after so stupidly
dissolving into tears over Ellie's letter. Oliver was the
kind of man who was compassionate to anyone in distress, but he wanted to believe that his comfort meant
something just a little bit special.

She lay on her back, her hand under her head, and
stared into the pale moonglow of night which gave an
eerie light through the window. Being so high up in the
building, and Riverside standing in its own grounds as it
did with no one overlooking it, she seldom drew the
curtains across. She'd need to in winter, she supposed.
Winter! It was hard to imagine now when the atmosphere was so humid, the days long and often tiring with
hours of unbroken sunshine. She would anxiously watch
the post after the next couple of days in anticipation of
some reply to her letter, so that she could arrange her
trip before summer was over. Suppose Oliver was right
and her grandfather was dead? His relations might not
be very pleased to hear from an old love, but Veronica
refused to allow her thoughts to be negative ones. She
felt in her bones that her grandfather was alive and
would be overjoyed to hear from her. Somewhere Betty
Smith was urging her on with her quest, and the influence of her mother was never far away.

Veronica just wished Oliver would give his blessing to
her efforts. She wanted to please him even if he didn't
notice her. As Natalie had so rightly said, the months
would fly by and in no time at all she would be thinking of

returning home. She sighed; she wouldn't want to go if she still felt as deeply about Oliver as she did now. It would be hell to have to leave him, but there was still—how many weeks? days? hours? She started to count . . .

Veronica hadn't set the alarm as she wasn't on duty until midday, and when she woke the sun almost blinded her as it shone directly on to her face. She stretched lazily and immediately her thoughts were of Oliver. She wished he was lying here with her, and she tortured herself with the memory of his delicate fingers tangling in her hair and smoothing her bare arms. Her flesh tingled with the ecstasy she had experienced—or was she dreaming? No, he had held her close to console her. Would she ever feel his lips on hers again? She didn't dare speculate, but no one could stop her loving him from a distance as she knew she would.

After breakfast she did some laundry, tidied her flat, and by the time she had showered, washed her hair and dressed ready for duty there was only time to take a brisk walk to the nearest shopping mall where she posted her letter, went to the bank and took an even brisker walk back to Riverside. The fresh air helped to clear her brain, and she resolved that she would telephone home at the earliest opportunity to tell her father and Ellie that at last she had taken some positive action. If she phoned now it would be very early in the morning in England, and she knew Ellie wasn't at her best before ten o'clock, so she decided to wait until she returned to her flat at nine o'clock that evening.

She prepared a cheese and ham roll which she ate much too rapidly, drank down a cup of instant coffee and left her flat thinking as she ran down the stairs that she was beginning to think of it as home. Up to now she hadn't dared to admit that she had been just a little bit homesick. That, if she were being totally honest, was the real reason for her resort to emotional tears yesterday. She didn't expect anyone to understand, she didn't fully understand herself, as she certainly wasn't the kind of

person who could put on an act of 'helpless little girl'
whenever it suited her convenience. It may have been
due to tiredness and the strain of worrying about carrying out her task, added to which was the shock of the
letters from home. Today, though, she felt quite light-
headed with excitement, and it was a beautiful day.
Traffic on the main road to Brookville was heavy,
requiring all her concentration, but she was soon pulling
into the staff's car-park, and after checking in and
reporting for duty she began tidying the Outpatients
Department ready for the afternoon clinics. Only one or
two patients still remained, having been for blood tests,
and were waiting to make further appointments, and at
last the department was clear. Veronica was checking on
lists and files when Dave joined her.

'Hullo there. Nice to have you back with us, I missed
you. Bet you're glad not to have Gloria breathing down
your neck?'

'I don't know why everyone has such a down on poor
Gloria, she isn't *that* bad,' protested Veronica.

'You can say that after what she did to you?'

'I stood up for myself, and once she'd found that I
could she wasn't likely to try it on again, was she? She
doesn't bother me, I think she's rather pathetic, especially as Mrs Walcott told me a bit about her background. I don't believe in making enemies if it can be
avoided.'

'It would be difficult to make an enemy out of you,
and—if what I heard this morning is true—you've even
got our esteemed consultant surgeon eating out of your
hand.' Dave smiled boyishly, but Veronica rounded on
him aggressively.

'Why are hospitals such notorious places for gossip-
mongering?' she said crossly. If you must know, I had a
letter from Ellie yesterday. They've found an old letter
from my grandfather, one of several actually, but this
one is significant because it seems my grandfather had
been patiently waiting for my grandmother to come to
America, and in this letter he finally gives up waiting and
tells her that he plans to marry someone else. It was so

sad, Dave, and when I met Oliver I just dissolved into tears. Pretty uncharacteristic of me, maybe I was extra tired or something, but he was very kind and understanding.'

'Oh, that's our Oliver, of course.' There was a hint of mockery in Dave's voice.

'Yes, it was typical of him, but you'd have reacted exactly the same way if I'd met you first. By the way, why weren't you at the barbecue?'

'On call, worse luck. Oliver doesn't often go to the social events, not if he can help it, but when he said he'd like to go I said I'd stand in—after all, he usually stands in for any of us on those occasions. It just so happened that Robert Olsen had a day off. You were seen to be canoodling in the trees and then you drove off together.'

'Not jealous, surely, Dave?' she laughed.

'Of course—I'm ever hopeful, Veronica, even though I know my chances are slim, but when you realise that Oliver doesn't get involved with the staff here you'll come running back to me—I hope!'

'Well, for your information we were not canoodling, he was consoling me, and when we left we went in our own cars—there, satisfied?' She gave him a playful poke.

'If you say so, but it's where you went that bothers me.'

'OK. Strictly between ourselves, though it's none of your damned business, or anyone else's for that matter, he suggested we had coffee at his place, which we did, and ended up arguing about Jenny Pearson.'

Dave stopped in his tracks and looked directly at Veronica with disbelief in his expression. Then at her knowing grin they both laughed together. 'You said he wouldn't approve,' she told Dave, 'and he doesn't—about reuniting Jenny with her father—fat chance of that anyway. He thinks it might create more problems for her, which in a way is right, I suppose, depending on what type of man he is, but somehow I have a sneaky suspicion that Mr Pearson might be the wronged party in all this. He must have felt something for his wife, to be at her funeral.'

'Could be idle curiosity—to get a glimpse of Jenny perhaps, or if I'm being cynical he might have been after anything that was going—like the house or money.'

'No, I don't think that,' Veronica said adamantly. 'He's evidently been in touch with the attorney over the house, but he doesn't seem to have caused Jenny any aggro at all. It appears to be hers to do as she likes with.'

'Just biding his time, I guess,' Dave said ruefully. As they stood side by side at the desk checking his list for the afternoon he suddenly put his arm around her waist and squeezed. Veronica twisted this way and that to escape his grasp, but no matter how she wriggled and begged him to stop he was determined to tease her. There was no one else around, so the horseplay developed into quite an exchange of physical contact, when Dave abruptly broke away. He ran his hand through his fair hair and Veronica watched an embarrassed flush creep slowly into his cheeks.

'Hullo, Oliver,' he said meekly.'

It was Veronica's turn to look abashed as one glimpse at Oliver's eyes burning with annoyance made her concentrate on the folders on the desk.

'I wasn't aware that we could afford playtimes for the staff at Brookville,' he said shortly, his handsome face dark with irritation.

CHAPTER SIX

VERONICA felt her stomach tighten. Oliver was the last person she wanted to witness any kind of frolic going on between herself and Dave, or anyone else for that matter. They weren't doing any harm, of course, the department was empty and they were preparing for the afternoon clinics, but from the expression on Oliver's face it was clear that he disapproved, and it vexed Veronica. Her cheeks were scarlet, not just with embarrassment but from the exertion she had needed to use to keep Dave at bay. It was just harmless fun, both she and Dave realised that, and she couldn't imagine why Oliver looked so disgusted.

'Killing time until the next onslaught,' Dave said now with a hint of impatience in his tone. 'What are you doing here anyway, Oliver? I thought I was doing your clinics today.'

'I was called out to see Mrs Walcott. She was having stomach pains and there was a bit of a flap on, but it was nothing. She'd over-indulged, I believe, with the food there. I suspect she's got used to eating bread, soup and biscuits at home when she's by herself and now that she's having everything done for her, and the place does have a good reputation where food is concerned, I rather think she's been making a pig of herself. Can't blame her really, but after surgery at her age she must be sensible. I have the feeling she's getting used to the life there. I'm hoping she may not want to return to her own home.'

'I wouldn't bank on that,' Dave said flatly. 'You know what the elderly are like about leaving their homes, and she's been more independent than most.'

Oliver was at his desk busily writing up Mrs Walcott's notes. Veronica watched him for a brief moment, noticing the way his wavy hair was brushed to perfection and shone when the light played on it. His hands moved silently over the pages, long elegant fingers with expertly manicured nails holding his pen tightly as he wrote his observations in neat handwriting. He paused, read through what he had written, and sat deep in thought, while Veronica felt her bosom swell with love for him. It was a senseless love, she knew, for he obviously didn't find her any more attractive than any other woman, and couldn't he have the pick of numerous sophisticated professional women? In her mind's eye she saw the picture of herself as she viewed it each time she looked in the mirror. She had pleasant features even if she wasn't a classic beauty and no way could she be called 'pretty', but her eyes were a good shape, large and sparkling green, though shaded with grey sometimes in her more solemn moods. Her rich-coloured hair accentuated the pale creaminess of her flawless skin, which could all too easily be turned to crimson as it had done a few moments ago.

Time seemed to have become motionless as she stood there looking and loving Oliver Linley, and then he glanced up, their souls mirrored through their eyes headed for a collision course which sent Veronica's heart fluttering wildly. He gazed at her unflinchingly with a deep emotional stare similar to the way he had looked at Maud, and Veronica blinked back to reality. He was confusing her with Maud, of course. She turned quickly, lest he notice the pain of her anguished heart, and went to assist Dave with setting up his examination tray. She fumbled with an instrument, dropped another, all the while aware of Oliver's eyes boring into her back. The blood had rushed into her cheeks, so she kept her back towards him, and presently she heard the scuff as he pushed his chair away from his desk. He hovered behind her for several seconds, then went to where Dave was busy refreshing his memory with the names of patients he was scheduled to see.

'I'll leave you to it, then,' said Oliver. 'By the way, you'll both be pleased to know that Jenny Pearson is in great shape and reiterating her wish to return to work. She's been marvellous company for Mrs Walcott, but having her own visitors seems to have been just what she needed. She asked after you both, so if you've got any off-duty together why don't you pop over to see her before she leaves for New Haven?'

Dave grinned at him. 'That's the best suggestion you've made in a long while—we might just do that. How about it, Veronica?'

'Yes, I'd like to see Jenny again, and Mrs Walcott too.' She dared to meet Oliver's piercing stare. He was saying so much in that 'telling' mannerism of his that she felt herself go hot and cold in turn. She only wished she knew him better so that she could interpret his meaning. He smiled suddenly, but instead of smiling back she turned her head away, and in an instant he had left the room. Now why had she done that? She felt so mad at herself that she started to do things with extra purpose and made quite a thing of plumping up the pillows in the examination cubicles. Dave came up behind her and held her shoulders firmly. 'Sorry, honey. I guess you'd rather he hadn't seen us horsing around together—but who knows, maybe it hasn't done any harm.'

'I don't know what you mean,' Veronica said aggressively.

'Oh, come on, Veronica, your eyes tell me what you're feeling, and he isn't blind either, you know.'

'Humph!' she said in contempt, 'he isn't interested in me, he's still carrying a torch for Maud Kishnev.'

'But that doesn't alter the way you feel for him. You're suffering from quite a bad case of lovesickness, and I'm sorry it's wasted on him. I know I'm a poor substitute, and as you know I'm rather keen on Jenny, but you can cry on my shoulder any time.'

'I don't want to cry on anyone's shoulder, thank you,' she answered decisively.

'You were willing to on Oliver's last evening,' Dave reminded her.

'That was different,' she snapped.

He gave a little lighthearted chuckle. 'I guess the tears could suit either purpose, but I don't like to see you unhappy, Veronica so how about a trip out to visit our ex-patients tomorrow?'

Veronica didn't answer immediately. She didn't want to sound too eager, but Dave was good company, he could make her laugh usually and she knew she would be doing him a favour by going along. He could hardly visit Jenny alone while she was still under Brookville's care. Veronica couldn't imagine whether anything was ever going to come of his infatuation for Jenny, though she had to admit that they were well matched. Dave's boyishness, his gentle, compassionate nature were just the thing Jenny needed in a relationship, and she felt hopeful that things might work out between them.

The afternoon clinics were not too busy. There was time to relax and the patients were not hurried, and when Veronica went off duty she felt unharassed, yet at the same time unsettled after seeing Oliver at midday. She wished she could have been going to visit Jenny and Mrs Walcott with him, but he was so involved with all departments in the hospital and probably many committees outside that sometimes days passed and she didn't even set eyes on him.

When she assisted Oliver at his clinic the following morning she felt considerably brighter, especially as he started off by greeting her cordially.

''Morning, Veronica. How's everything? No news yet? No follow-up to your letter?'

'No, it's a bit soon, I suppose. I keep hoping for a phone call, yet I'd be apprehensive if there was one. I did manage to get through to home last evening, but Ellie was out and Dad didn't seem to be interested in Mum's father. I'm not sure whether he genuinely wasn't feeling too well, or whether it's the effects of Ellie looking after him, but he seemed down.'

'I'm sorry—and there's not much you can do from so far away. Are you worried?'

Veronica shook her head. 'Not much point in worrying when there's so little I can do. I'll write him a long letter soon to make up for my lack of communication. He's always hated the telephone and it may have been

that he was watching a favourite programme on television or was doing something that he didn't want to be
disturbed at. He couldn't think of anything much to tell
me, and of course I was more interested in the letters
they'd found. He's never been too keen on the idea of
trying to trace my grandfather, and he did warn me from
the beginning that the authorities aren't too helpful. I
might almost say that I think he was disappointed they
unearthed these letters, while Ellie and I are quite
excited about it.'

'Pity your sister was out,' commented Oliver.
'Perhaps you picked a bad time to phone—but don't say
that I too haven't warned you, Veronica. I don't want to
have to come to your rescue.'

'I'm sure that won't be necessary, Oliver. I won't let
my perseverance interfere with my work.'

'But you'll go heading off to Rochester at the drop of a
hat, and I feel responsible for you.'

'Then please don't. I'm quite capable of looking after
myself.'

'So you keep telling me, but America isn't quite like
the UK. It's very large and can be very unfriendly.'

'I haven't found it so,' she retorted with a toss of her
head.

He raised his head and accosted her with an intense
stare until the beautiful blue shade of his eyes calmed her
stubborn spirit. 'You've forgotten so soon?' he queried
softly.

Veronica shifted awkwardly from one foot to the
other. 'Well, no, I know I was grateful for your help at
Kennedy, but airports anywhere can be like that, and
I'm sure I shall always manage to find a guardian angel to
see me through.'

A smile, not his usual 'telling' one, but a genuine
warm expression of amusement, lit up his face and
wrinkles appeared at the corners of his eyes. 'A-h,' he
mused, 'so that's how you see me, is it? Your guardian
angel?' He inclined his head and was obviously satisfied
with his own thoughts. 'How will you tell whether
someone is an authentic guardian angel or an abductor?'

'Oh, really, Oliver, you're just trying to frighten me! I don't even know that I'm going to Rochester yet. My letter may be completely ignored.'

'And that, I fancy, will only make you the more determined to go there. Please don't do anything rash without consulting me. I've noticed that you already have several days off saved up.'

'It seemed the sensible thing to do, whether I go to Rochester or not. I daren't go home without seeing,' she shrugged, 'mm . . . Disney World, the Grand Canyon?'

'You've got a lot of living to do before your year is up, Veronica. Let's not talk about you going home yet awhile.' There might almost have been a sadness in his eyes as he said this. But no, Veronica told herself, she was just imagining things. Nursing staff came and went, and all Oliver did was his duty as director of Brookville. He was only being paternal about her because she happened to be from England. 'I think maybe we ought to see—er—Timothy James?' His eyebrows were raised, and she went outside and called the patient's name.

On the whole she enjoyed working with Oliver, especially when he was in a relaxed frame of mind as he appeared to be today, and she was almost disappointed when Natalie came to relieve her.

'Are we nearly through?' the head nurse asked.

'Yes, it's been quite an easy clinic. Timothy James has been for blood tests and will be coming back to see Oliver again. Suspected appendix; Oliver said he might have him in straight away if there are no complications. Poor little chap, he's only six.'

'Better to get it done and over with if that's the problem. Anything else I should know?'

Veronica went through the list and then left the department in Natalie's capable hands.

She drove back to Riverside wondering whether Dave was still at Brookville as she hadn't seen him all day, but he could have been on the wards, in the theatre or busy elsewhere. She showered and changed, then prepared sandwiches and tea, but still Dave did not appear. She

switched off the kettle and went downstairs to his apartment, but after knocking on the door twice and getting
no reply she was on the way upstairs again when she
heard his cheery whistle. She turned and sat on the
stairs, waiting until he came into the hallway.

'Had a busy day?' she asked innocently.

'Not bad,' he grinned in his usual unflappable way.
'I'm a bit later than I meant to be. You look as if you're
all ready?'

'Tea and sandwiches before you change?' she asked.

'Mm, sounds just what the doctor ordered; bless you,
Veronica. I'll be with you in about ten minutes.'

Veronica went back to her flat and made the tea, by
which time Dave had arrived. They sat and enjoyed their
refreshment in a leisurely manner before setting off
for the luxurious grounds and large house where Mrs
Walcott and Jenny Pearson were staying.

'This is so peaceful,' Veronica said as she got out of
the car. 'What beautiful surroundings!'

Dave agreed, and together they went into the large
tile-floored hall. Almost at once a smart middle-aged
woman came to meet them. 'I'm Mrs Curtiss. I expect
you're Veronica Summers and Dave Wilfroy? Dr Linley
told me to expect you. Mrs Walcott is feeling much
better now, and Jenny can hardly wait to go home,
though we're pressing her to remain for her scheduled
two weeks.'

'I'm not surprised she's so much better,' said Veronica. 'It's so relaxing here, and I'm sure Mrs Walcott
won't want to go home.'

'It isn't very often I get a dissatisfied client, but
occasionally one will try to find fault, but I have to admit
both Jenny and old Mrs Walcott have been very good
patients. They spend a great deal of their time sitting in
the communal sun-room overlooking the small lake.
Jenny finds the stories Mrs Walcott tells most amusing,
some unbelievable, and Mrs Walcott in turn has been a
good listening post for Jenny to get all her past worries
out into the open.' As she spoke Mrs Curtiss led the way
through a corridor into a very large lounge where French

windows opened out into a glass sun-room with sliding doors to the patio and garden. Some elderly folk were sleeping, others walking by the lake, but they found Mrs Walcott and Jenny sitting on the patio enjoying drinks of red grape juice.

'Will you look at this?' teased Dave, bringing a bright flush to Jenny's cheeks. 'Living it up, eating too much, drinking before supper to get up an appetite?' He shook his head in mock disapproval. 'I think we'll have to have these patients back at Brookville to keep an eye on them.'

Old Mrs Walcott winked saucily at Veronica as her sunken eyes flitted from the handsome Dave to Jenny. 'Well, Jenny may be willing, but you can forget about sending me anywhere,' she said. 'We don't want to see no more doctors and nurses, only our *friends*, isn't that right, Jenny?'

'It's lovely to see you both,' Jenny said, laughing happily. Veronica was delighted to see how well she had progressed, and Dave pulled up chairs close by and almost before they could sit down Mrs Curtiss came out bringing a tray of drinks and small savoury biscuits for the guests. 'Supper is a light meal, so you can join us if you like?' she invited.

Veronica was about to say that they had eaten when Dave intervened quickly with: 'That's very good of you, we'd love to, wouldn't we, Veronica?' She smiled in acknowledgement and took the glass of red grape juice she was offered. Mrs Curtiss passed a few pleasantries with Dave, then left.

'Now then, let's hear all the news,' he asked Jenny.

'I don't have to tell you how wonderful I feel,' she began. 'It's like staying in a hotel. We're not pressurised in any way, are we, Mrs Walcott?'

'We-ell . . . no, not quite like at Brookville, though I have to confess I had no complaints about the treatment there. Here we're persuaded to get off our backsides and do things for ourselves—in the kindest way, of course. It's different for young Jenny, she's fully recovered and has her life before her. There'll be no stopping her now that her friends have been to see her—such a nice young man came.'

'Now hold on, don't get the wrong idea,' protested Jenny. 'Mrs Walcott is trying to marry me off quickly to the first eligible bachelor who shows up! Ron Golding brought his wife and teenage girls to visit, which I thought was great of him, and Bryan Coates came along too. I work with these two guys and I like them both, but that's all there is to it, really,' she said, aiming to convince Dave.

'It was nice of them to come to see you, Jenny,' said Veronica. 'It'll make returning to work so much easier, won't it?'

'Just talking shop for a short while made me realise how dreadfully lazy I've been over these past few weeks. I'm going to love going back, and then I'm considering making a clean break from Groton and moving house down to New Haven.'

'Ooh!' Dave said gravely. 'I don't know that I can allow that—I mean, isn't it a bit soon to be making rash decisions? Once you've moved, you've moved!'

Jenny laughed lightheartedly. 'That's the whole idea, Dave,' she said, glancing at Veronica, 'and you approve, don't you, Veronica?'

'I'd rather not commit myself. I would advise caution, though. Yes, I think Dave is right, don't rush into anything until you're back at work and coping with the outside world again. You may have days when everything seems an effort, we all do, but take your time to get back into the swing of things.'

'Don't worry, my solicitor won't let me do anything silly, and selling house takes time anyway,' said Jenny. 'I shall be seeing Dr Linley once more before I return to work, so I'll see what he thinks of the idea.'

'Our advice not good enough for you?' said Dave in mock disappointment.

'You know I didn't mean that,' Jenny said, reaching forward and placing her hand over Dave's. 'I owe so much to all of you, and Mrs Walcott, who refuses to let me be glum and self-pitying. I shan't move until I know where she's going and that she's OK. We're going to keep in touch—I've declared her my adoptive mother.'

Veronica noticed Mrs Walcott's eyes brimming as the old lady took Jenny's hand in hers. In spite of her advanced years and her occasional sharp tongue she had been as much help in Jenny's rehabilitation as anyone, and it had drawn them so close together, they were like mother and daughter, or perhaps grandmother and granddaughter! Veronica felt a strange cold feeling flood through her veins as she thought of her own grandfather whom she was searching for. She was almost pleased when Mrs Walcott said: 'Now then, young Dr Wilfroy, why don't you let Jenny show you round the grounds here while Veronica tells me all about what she's been up to?'

Dave looked questioningly first at Jenny, then at Veronica.

'Yes, a good idea—go on,' Veronica urged. 'I'm going to tell Mrs Walcott about the latest development in my quest.'

'But I want to hear too,' Jenny protested.

'There she goes again, passing me up for someone else!' But Dave was already on his feet, and Jenny quickly followed.

Veronica and Mrs Walcott followed their progress with interest as Jenny gazed up into Dave's eyes with shared admiration, and it wasn't long before Dave had grasped Jenny's hand firmly in his. 'There goes one very contented young lady,' Mrs Walcott said in her husky matter-of-fact tone. 'She hardly seems the same girl now. Must have been some real good blood you put into her, that's for sure!'

'Anaemia is a most unpleasant thing,' Veronica told her. 'A few people might notice that the patient is pale and listless, but sometimes even a doctor can miss it. Poor Jenny, she deserves some happiness—I only wish her father would show up. Oliver won't hear of us trying to contact him, but I'm sure it's just what Jenny needs.'

Mrs Walcott ruminated over this for a few minutes, then she said: 'I can understand his reticence, Veronica.

He hasn't bothered all this time, and they'd be like strangers, most likely. We don't know all the facts, though Jenny has talked a great deal about her mother and I fancy she was pretty demanding even when she wasn't ill. Possessive—much more'n a mother should be with a daughter of over twenty. She should have thought how Jenny was going to cope alone when she was gone. Mebbe she didn't plan on leaving just yet, but she should have looked to the future.'

'Jenny has nothing to reproach herself with, but the finality of death does take some coming to terms with, and I had Dad and Ellie as well as other members of the family,' said Veronica. 'I just wish there was someone Jenny could turn to.'

'Wouldn't you say she just has found a good friend?' Mrs Walcott tapped her nose knowingly. 'And I feel they're right for each other.'

'Oh, Mrs Walcott, they hardly know each other yet!'

'When you get to my age, my dear, you're gifted with a second sight of sorts. That young man had designs on you and any other pretty miss who came his way at first, but I watched his reaction to Jenny, and his concern was more personal than being her doctor. It was a gradual attraction, and often that's best. Young Dr Wilfroy has changed too, I'd say he's less ambitious and more looking to becoming a family man.'

Veronica couldn't quite see Dave in that role just yet, but she knew what the wise Mrs Walcott meant, and she was glad for Jenny. Their conversation soon disgressed from Dave and Jenny when the couple were out of sight, and Veronica told Mrs Walcott about the letters her father and Ellie had found.

'I'm so anxious to go to Rochester that I'll be terribly disappointed now if my grandfather is dead,' she said wistfully.

'Finding lost relatives is no easy thing, especially in a different country, and there must be hundreds of women who'd like nothing better than to meet up with their American fathers, but the authorities don't like handing out names and addresses for one reason and another. It's nothing personal, Veronica, but a long-lost child can cause some strong feelings in some families, not to mention breaking up marriages. I understand that you must do what you came to do, but don't be too upset if you aren't welcomed with open arms.'

'I've got it all worked out,' Veronica said thoughtfully, appreciating what Mrs Walcott was trying to say. 'At first if I find any of his family I shall simply say that my grandmother met Burt Duvall and appears to have corresponded with him during and after the war. They can't take offence at that, can they?'

The old lady pursed her thin, cracked lips and agreed. 'I shall be interested to hear whether or not you get to find anyone,' she said kindly, and then as Dave and Jenny came into view a supper gong sounded. It was a pleasant visit, and on the return journey Dave was unusually silent, while Veronica was preoccupied with confused thoughts about Mrs Walcott as well as speculation concerning Jenny and Dave. The days passed by with no news at all, and Veronica experienced some melancholy. Her letter had not fallen on fruitful ground, which meant that the recipient was not interested. If the addressee was unknown she expected her letter to be returned to her as she had put her name and address on the back of the envelope, but three weeks passed with no news. Even after an evening out with her friends she felt very down one morning as she went on duty, which resulted in her being less attentive to Oliver's wishes as usual, but he refrained from commenting until the clinic was finished.

'Come into my office and close the door, Veronica,' he said abruptly. She followed meekly, not really aware that she hadn't been concentrating, but she guessed by his voice that something was amiss. She couldn't meet his gaze as he held the door open for her and she found her hand collide with his as she turned to shut the door at the same time as he. Then she saw that his eyes were warm and understanding rather than sharply critical. 'I gather from your black mood that you've had no response from your letter to Rochester?' he said, setting a chair behind her and indicating that she should sit.

'No, not yet,' she said, suddenly finding a defiant
spirit. 'It might take time, and I wasn't aware that I was
in a black mood.'

'Oh, come off it, Veronica,' he said in mock reproach.
'You haven't really been part of my team at all this
morning. I'm not complaining about your work—you're
so experienced you can do everything like a robot, but
I'd like to *feel* that you're with me—at least on my side
when I'm talking to patients.'

'I'm sorry,' she apologised humbly. 'You should have
reminded me sooner.'

'Reminded you of what, Veronica?' Oliver asked
gently. 'That you're my assistant, that you're here for
the benefit of the patients, or that I like to have your
attention—more than that, Veronica, I hoped we could
share confidences.'

She sat awkwardly on her chair. How could she
answer that, for goodness' sake?

'Is it really getting you down?' Oliver pursued.

'No! Well, I suppose I do feel disappointed that
there's been no reply yet,' she admitted. 'I was hoping
for a telephone call. I keep putting off ringing home in
the hope that I shall eventually have some news for
them.'

He smiled in his own inimitable way. 'Poor Veronica,'
he commiserated, making her feel she was behaving like
a pathetically unhappy child. 'I can sympathise, but in
such matters one has to be more than a little patient.
What would you say to a day out to try to cheer you up?
No, I'm not offering to take you to Rochester, but you're
not taking your full quota of off-duty and I feel you
should have some time away from Brookville.'

'But the hours are so good here. I'm certainly not
overworked, and I do go out—the girls took me to
Mystic yesterday evening to the Aquarium and village.'

'Good, so that's one place I can cross off my list. What
did you think of it?'

'Very interesting. The Aquarium is so clean and the
dolphin show excellent. I didn't realise that Mystic

village is in working order, if you know what I mean. I actually changed some traveller's cheques at the bank there.'

'Mystic itself is a nice place to shop. Did you get to see the seaport?'

'No, I'll need a whole day for that, I think. Natalie told me how it's all been preserved as it was years ago.'

'Mm . . . anywhere special that you'd like to go? No, how can you choose when you don't know what we have to offer? A mystery tour? How's that for imagination, Veronica? Ten o'clock tomorrow morning suit you?'

'But I'm on duty in the morning,' she told him.

'I'll OK that with Natalie. If you should hear from your people in Rochester or wherever they may have moved to you can have some time off then. Meanwhile I think you need cheering up, so we'll look forward to a day out, and pray for fine weather.'

Veronica glanced out of the window. 'It's been lovely for the past few weeks,' she said. 'Is it likely to change?'

'Getting a bit humid again so there might be a storm, but not tomorrow, we hope.' Oliver stood up and putting his arm around her waist walked her to the door, but paused before he turned the knob. She could feel his warm breath against her cheek and all thoughts of her grandfather were momentarily forgotten. His fingers squeezed her slim waist gently and she stifled a giggle, loving the contact yet wishing he would let her go. 'You always smell so deliciously . . . mm . . . English,' he murmured into her hair, and because she was in danger of losing her cap she inadvertently knocked his thigh as she tried to raise her hand. Oliver caught her fingers in his own and toyed with them as he stole a swift kiss on the side of her cheek. 'Just to get you in the mood for tomorrow, sweet Veronica—now be off with you and let me concentrate on my work.' She was never quite sure whether what she felt on her bottom was a pinch, a pat or a sensual squeeze, but whatever it was made her feel giddy with excitement at the thought of what was to come the following day.

CHAPTER SEVEN

VERONICA hardly slept at all; her brain was too busy fantasising about the proposed day out with Oliver. Would he back out at the last moment as he had before? Surely Maud Kishnev couldn't intrude a second time? Could she? Veronica was too fearful that something or someone was bound to put paid to her having him alone for a few hours that she gave no thought as to what she would wear until she was actually up and showered. She surveyed the contents of her wardrobe critically, wishing she had brought a number of items which were hanging up at home and which Ellie was probably making good use of in her absence.

It was a lovely morning, the sky blue, the sun high and full of promise. Should it be a sun-dress, or an all-purpose cotton one? A trouser suit even, made of crisp linen-type material, or . . . ? She sighed as she rummaged through the few things on the rail, then she selected a short-sleeved dress which had bold blue flowers on a white background. The skirt was full but not billowing, and the bodice fitted her trim figure snugly, the wide heart-shaped neckline showing off her mild tan which contrasted with the white beads she fastened round her neck, and the small matching button ear-rings which complemented her dainty ears. She didn't go in for much make-up usually, and today was no exception, just a light touch of pinkish lipstick and her cheeks protected from the sun with some expensive moisturising cream, then a spray of equally expensive perfume behind her ears, in her cleavage, on wrists and daringly behind her knees. She sniffed, hoping she hadn't overdone it, but when she sat on the side of the bed and secured the straps on her white sandals she got quite a whiff of it, so she twirled her skirt this way and that a few times in the hope that the scent would fade. It surely would once she was out in the open air, she tried to convince herself, and she was just checking that her white shoulder bag contained everything that any self-respecting girl should carry with her when the doorbell sounded clear and alert. Panic seized her—this was it! Dave had come to give her a message, and here she was looking like an overdressed wedding-guest! There was no time to change, only time to put on the casual white jacket of the same textured material as the dress when the doorbell pealed a second time with impatience.

She went to the door and opened it on the chain. That way she need not expose too much of herself, but it wasn't Dave who stood on the landing, it was Oliver, looking extremely attractive in grey lightweight slacks with a sky-blue shirt with matching grey flashes on the shoulders, stripes of varying widths across the chest, shoulders and at the edges of the short sleeves, and the neck open to reveal much more of Oliver's bronzed skin than Veronica had ever seen before. Even his eyes seemed to match the colour of his shirt and his expression was one of bright anticipation.

'Why the chain, for heaven's sake? You surely aren't anticipating assault and rape at this hour? And you should have been expecting me.'

Veronica closed the door together to allow her to slide back the chain. It gave her time to compose herself, to stay the rapid beating of her heart and destroy the burning doubt which must be etched in her expression.

'I was just being cautious,' she said. 'After all, you're earlier than you said and I'm barely ready. Besides . . .' her cheeks flushed awkwardly and she turned to lead the way into the lounge.

'Besides what?' Oliver prompted, then with an understanding nod he added: 'You thought I might let you down again as I was forced to do when Maud came to Groton. Well, I can't blame you for being suspicious, but I do assure you, my dear Veronica, that I don't willingly let down a pretty girl unless I'm obliged to, and I did explain about that.'

'And I quite understood,' she answered flatly, 'but

today was arranged rather speedily, so I felt I should be prepared for anything that might turn up at the last minute.'

Oliver smiled and looked her up and down. 'That's why I'm early, and I suggest we hit the road before someone discovers where I am.'

Veronica wasn't sure she liked the suggestion of his not being found at Riverside in her apartment, but she knew well enough what he meant. 'Are you expecting to be wanted?' she asked.

'Only by you,' came the swift banter, and she was compelled to laugh with the incorrigible Oliver Linley. 'Dave is on duty with Bob Olsen, so I can leave everything in their capable hands. There are plenty of specialists in most fields in the area if they need a second opinion. For once I can truthfully say I feel free of any real worries where my patients are concerned. Mrs Walcott is on my mind quite a bit, but there isn't a lot I can do for her now except be around if she needs me.'

'We thought she seemed pretty good,' Veronica said, 'and she was quite happy with Mrs Curtiss.'

Oliver had remained standing by the door, which was not quite closed. He pulled it open and indicated that he was eager to be off. 'Yes, she does seem quite content, but now that Jenny has left and is completely discharged I wonder how the old lady will fare.'

Veronica picked up her bag, checked that she had her key and followed him out.

'It really is good news that Jenny has found her confidence again,' she said. 'I'm sure everything will work out well for her now.'

Oliver paused on the stairs and whispered: 'And that's the last comment on Brookville and its patients for the rest of the day.' He waved a warning finger at her. 'It's our day off—remember?'

'Where are we going?' she asked.

'A mystery tour, I said, didn't I?'

'I wasn't sure what to wear.'

She heard him chuckle and murmur: 'You'll do very nicely—very nicely indeed.'

Veronica could have taken this either way, but she decided to give up worrying and try to enjoy his company. She sat beside him in his luxurious car and was pleased to be chauffeur-driven for a change. He seemed so relaxed behind the wheel, even though the traffic was heavy as they took the road towards the Thames river and across the bridge, past East and Old Lyme to pick up a northerly route.

'Do you happen to be a fan of Sherlock Holmes?' he asked.

'Not specially, why?'

'You have watched films and TV series, though?'

'Of course, Dad's a great fan.'

Oliver glanced across at her with a grin. 'I'd rather be taking you out than your father,' he said, 'but I think you'll find Gillette Castle interesting.'

They travelled through rural countryside and soon Veronica saw the signpost directing them to Gillette Castle. Oliver pulled into a spacious car-park, but he made no attempt to get out at first.

'I don't suppose you've ever heard of it,' he said. 'The first actor to ever play the part of Sherlock Holmes was the late William Gillette. He's well known for giving over a thousand performances of the famous detective throughout the world, and when he was looking for a site to build his castle said that this plot overlooking the Connecticut River was as beautiful as any he'd seen anywhere. In fact it reminded him of the Rhine Valley in Germany.'

Veronica felt his eyes taking in every detail of her profile. She was at a loss to know what to say, in spite of her interest in the castle and the man who built it. She had been acutely aware of the man who was giving her so much attention, and she was almost afraid of saying or doing something that might spoil the day. Since coming to the States she had found herself thinking back over the past to times spent with men friends who would have been happy to share a more intimate relationship with her, and she occasionally wondered whether she had been foolish in letting them all slip through her fingers, but now she knew the difference in her innermost feelings. Her heart was full to bursting with something so deep she was afraid of herself, something she had never experienced before.

As soon as he spoke she knew that Oliver had taken her silence to mean that she wasn't that interested in the Castle. He sighed and opened the car door. 'Well, since we're here you may as well see the scenery if nothing else.' He slammed his door shut so hard that the car rocked, and while he was locking it she got out too, and over the roof she faced him. 'Oliver, it's very good of you to give up your valuable time like this for me,' she said pointedly. 'The weather is so gorgeous—and the air——' she spread her hands out in a meaningful gesture. 'I feel that perhaps there was something else you might have preferred to do on your day off.'

At first he looked quite solemn, then the laughter lines appeared at the corner of his eyes even though he was trying to prevent a smile escaping. 'There is something else I want to do—but not here,' he told her.

Veronica knew that the colour had suffused her cheeks at his hidden implication. Desire was in his every look and movement and he knew she felt more than a little interested in his feelings. Slowly, his footsteps crunching on the gravel drive, he walked round to her side and stood very close as he locked her door. 'We're going to have a good day together, Veronica, and there's nothing I want better than to be spending it with you.' He took her arm and led her towards the impressive-looking building. 'Not a medieval castle like we have at home,' he explained as they queued up for tickets.

'But very distinctive,' she said as she browsed through the guidebook which Oliver bought, 'and I'm grateful to you for bringing me to see something so elegant and which I'd never heard of—but 1913 isn't so old, is it?'

'No, but it's quite a unique masterpiece with massive stone walls, five feet thick, which took a crew of twenty-two masons five years to construct.'

Beautiful plants and shrubs climbed over the exterior, and inside Veronica was intrigued to learn that Gillette had designed everything himself, even to the hand-carved doors with their intricate locking systems, and in his study a desk slid back and forth on metal runners, just a sample of many clever inventions by the actor-owner of the Castle.

'How do you feel about cats?' asked Oliver.

'Not as besotted as William Gillette evidently was, judging by the numerous paintings and drawings, not to mention the cat doorstops!'

'And the collection of ceramic cats, some quite bizarre,' Oliver pointed out. They became engrossed in the unusual house with the inventor's many secret gadgets, and out into the sunshine once more Oliver led Veronica down to the river where they ambled along in the growing heat of midday. 'That's far enough,' he said. 'It's quite a climb back up to the car-park.' But although breathless, Veronica was enjoying herself too much to mind the heat, and Oliver kept his hand firmly at her back to help her up the steep winding path. 'I don't think you need this,' he said, drawing the light jacket back from her shoulders, and he insisted on carrying it for her. In the seclusion of a bend in the pathway he bent and kissed her neck. 'You're looking very attractive, darling. Forgive me for commenting, but I can't understand why you're still unattached.'

Veronica smiled up at him wistfully. 'Because I want to be, I suppose.'

His hand slid away from her waist as if she had said something to indicate that she didn't like being touched. 'A bad experience, perhaps?' he said as much to himself as to her.

'Oh, no, Oliver, nothing like that. I've had lots of friends, but no one who was ever special enough for me to consider becoming really attached.'

It seemed that this was not sufficient explanation to allow him to return to his amiable attitude, and as they reached the top of the path he said: 'Let's go in the cafeteria for a cup of coffee.'

Veronica drank hers to drown her drooping spirit. The earlier magic had vanished and she supposed she

had said the wrong thing again, but as they drove on
through country roads Oliver was soon chatting happily,
and when they reached another part of the river at East
Haddam he showed her the Goodspeed Opera House
where many famous stars had performed. By the time he
had walked her round the area it was time for lunch, and
they sat in a garden café to enjoy a tuna platter while
overlooking the river, and Veronica was fascinated by
the design of the bridge which, instead of lifting up to
enable tall masts to pass underneath it, divided in the
centre, one half swinging one way and the other half in
the opposite direction to make a passage through.

'There's always so much to watch near the sea or a
river,' said Veronica as she tucked into her delicious fish
salad.

'And this New England isn't so very different from our
own England, is it? After all, the pioneers came from
home, which is why so many places bear the same names
which are so familiar to us. I bet you never expected to
find a River Thames and a New London here, unless
you'd done your homework before you left?'

Veronica raised her eyebrows with a touch of guilt. 'I
wish I could say I had,' she confessed, 'but my chief
concern was to find out how far away Rochester was
from Groton.'

'Mm . . . and you've discovered it's not too far at all
by courtesy of easy travelling here in the States?'

'Far enough, and what might I discover when I get
there? I know,' she went on, 'you'd prefer me not to go,
but I'll never be able to live with myself if I don't, being
this close.'

'As long as you make all the necessary arrangements
properly and in good time. Don't rush into anything,
Veronica, I don't want to see you get hurt.'

'But you still think I shall be hurting someone else?'

'I . . . I know the past can be most intriguing, but the
authorities do sometimes know best,' he said gently.
'Sadly your mother and grandmother are both dead, so
who is this mission going to benefit?'

'My grandfather, if he's still alive.'

'But possibly upset his family. No, Veronica, I can't say I'm happy about the project at all, but the decision has to be yours—if you ever hear from anyone in Rochester. They may have moved long since, and I rather hope they have.'

'We'll just have to wait and see,' she said, not wanting to spoil the day by embarking on an argument concerning her future activities.

They fell into an easy silence as they sipped their coffee. A noisy party of youngsters queued to order their lunch and then spread themselves around the unoccupied tables, laughing and horsing around, so Oliver smiled and said: 'Drink up and we'll be off.'

Veronica bought a few souvenirs and picture postcards of the area before they went back to the car. It was really hot now and she felt quite tired, so she settled back in her seat and enjoyed the drive through country roads, though she had no idea where they were going or where she was, unless Oliver pointed out some landmark or interesting building. When they reached the coast he pulled into the car-park at Rocky Neck State Park. 'A walk now to work off your lunch.' He turned and smiled at her. 'I have a distinct feeling that you were about to go to sleep on me,' he laughed.

'I was hoping you wouldn't notice,' she said. 'You shouldn't have dined and wined me so well.'

'I should have told you to bring your swimming things. The beach here is a bit crowded, though, so we'll walk in the woods and see what we can find.'

Veronica was surprised to find that he was as knowledgeable about trees, shrubs and rare plants as he was about medicine. He sauntered along, more interested in what was on the ground than in her, then he suddenly stopped. 'Come here,' he commanded. Veronica went to where he had bent low and saw that between his fingers he was holding an exquisite pink bloom. 'I wish I could pick one for you, but it's a protected species, thank goodness. Do you know what it is?'

'I'm not much up in such things,' she confessed, 'but it looks similar to an orchid.'

'Well done, that's exactly what it is—a wild one, named My Lady's Slipper, quite rare and beautiful, so we only talk about it in whispers.'

'It so tiny and delicate it's hardly noticeable. Anyone could walk on one without seeing it.'

'Which is why we have to keep to the paths. The only chance of finding one is if they happen to be growing near the path, and today we were lucky.' Voices drew nearer shortly afterwards, so Oliver held Veronica's arm and they strolled on, coming out to the park which skirted the beach, where a long neck of rocks stretched out into the sea. They sat on a grassy bank and gazed out to the open waters where water-skiers skimmed the glistening mirror and yachts gently manoeuvred in the slight breeze.

'The public are very well catered for with barbecue facilities here,' Veronica observed.

'Yes, it's a favourite picnic spot, particularly at weekends. Parks in America are rather different from back home, but then there are such wide open spaces everywhere for people to spread.' He was thoughtful for a few moments, then he looked across at her with hidden meaning in his expression. Veronica couldn't begin to understand what he might be thinking, then he said casually: 'Are we ready to move?'

She took this to mean that the day had ended as far as the outing was concerned, so she got to her feet hastily. 'It's been very pleasant,' she said. 'I'd never know how to find these beauty spots by myself.'

'And I'd be very angry if you attempted to go off exploring by yourself, my girl.' He put his arm around her waist as they returned to the car-park. 'And the day is far from over yet,' he said softly in her ear as she took her place in the front passenger seat.

Veronica assumed that he was taking her back to Riverside, but they went off the beaten track through a long, winding, leafy lane, where after travelling for what seemed to Veronica about a mile he turned into a wide entrance, coming to rest in front of an open garage which was at one end of a spacious low bungalow, half hidden by tall trees. Veronica hoped her sudden intake of breath wasn't audible as she realised with a rush of excitement where he had brought her.

'Welcome to Linley's hideaway,' he said, undoing his seat belt and releasing the catch on hers. At his bidding she got out of the car and stood looking in awe at his luxurious home, remembering that this was where he brought Maud when she visited Groton, which clouded her vision somewhat.

'I'm sure you could do with a cup of tea as much as I need one,' said Oliver, leading the way into the kitchen where heavy oak beams ran the length of the ceiling. He went to one of the long worktops and switched the kettle on, then took two mugs down from the mug tree in the corner. It was far too elegant for a mere bachelor, Veronica decided. In spite of it being in the mode of a farmhouse kitchen everything was clean-looking with plenty of modern equipment—a woman's dream, she thought enviously.

'So you like my kitchen?' he asked as he went to the huge fridge-freezer and fetched milk and a plate of fresh dairy cream cakes.

'Who wouldn't?' she said dreamily.

'Some women might prefer an ultra-modern all-white kitchen, but for me I like warmth and homeliness. Please be honest, if you don't care for my tastes say so.'

'But I love it, Oliver,' she responded eagerly. 'It's large and well designed, and it looks out on to the garden, which is so beautifully rural,' she enthused. 'Can't you just see children playing there?'

Oliver paused long enough to look from the garden back to her with great interest, or was it fear? She realised that what she had said might make him think she had designs on him—well, she did, but he must never suspect.

'Yours? he queried with a lopsided grin. 'Mine? Ours?'

Veronica shrugged. 'Anyone's,' she said simply.

'Are you implying that this is all wasted on a mere bachelor?'

'Certainly not—but I doubt that you'll remain a bachelor for ever.'

Oliver raised a sleek eyebrow. 'All a question of fate, I expect, don't you?' She watched as he poured water on to the tea-bags in the teapot, then he held his arm out to her. 'Come on, while the tea brews I'll show you the rest of the rooms, and you may like to freshen up.'

He started with the largest front room, which was the master bedroom, complete with shower-room en-suite. There was nothing lying about to indicate that anyone lived in the place, Veronica thought. She wished there was a tie hanging over the mirror on the light oak dressing table, or a dressing-gown on the back of the door, a pair of slippers even, but the décor was plain and simple, the accent on the genuine wood of the furniture, and nothing was out of place.

'A bit unlived-in, I expect you're thinking,' Oliver said. 'A woman comes in to look after everything so it's kept tidy and clean, but I should use the place more, I know.'

'It's rather isolated out here, isn't it?' she questioned, looking out of the second bedroom window and seeing nothing but trees. 'There must be neighbours somewhere close by, surely?'

'Just the other side of those shrubs. Another doctor and his wife and three girls, and on the other side of the garage there's a smaller property where a retired policeman and his family live, so I'm not as isolated as you might think. It's the privacy I like, though, and need.' He showed her where the bathroom was and left her to freshen up, after which she returned to the large lounge where he had taken the tea and cakes.

'I hope you're hungry again,' he said, offering her a cream cake.

'We-ell,' she said with doubt in her voice, 'I really didn't . . .'

'Oh, go on, spoil yourself, you'll work it all off at work tomorrow.'

Veronica sank her teeth into delicious choux pastry oozing with cream and watched Oliver watching her with amusement in his eyes. 'I should have provided you with a fork or something,' he said, studying his own.

'They taste much nicer like this,' she managed to say, knowing she must look like a messy child at a party.

'A serviette at least,' he said, and went to the sideboard to fetch some.

Conversation wasn't really practical until the cakes had been eaten with relish, which gave Veronica the opportunity to take in his masculine lounge. The dominant colour was a deep blue on carpet and plain walls, but the covers on the settee and easy chairs, of which there were a large number, was blue also but complemented with a design of huge pale lemon flowers with green foliage. A similar floral pattern was repeated in the velvet curtains which hung to floor length. It was different from anything she would either have imagined or chosen herself, but it was most effective and created a cosy atmosphere.

'How long have you lived here?' she asked after she had cleaned up the results of her indulgence with the serviette.

'About two years. It's fairly old and had been allowed to fall into disrepair, so it's been a kind of hobby to make it habitable. When you've finished your tea we'll go downstairs.'

'Downstairs?' she queried.

'Yes, most properties in America and Canada are built with cellars. A useful asset to take refuge in during hurricanes—and they do occur, the most notable being in 1938.'

'Oh, yes, 1938, that brings back memories—or at least it would if Mrs Walcott were here. It appears to be the one catastrophe which no one forgets, and the new generations aren't being allowed to either.'

Oliver laughed heartily. 'Talk to anyone who was around at the time and you'll certainly get the full story! At Ocean Beach the waterfront was completely ravaged, sand covered everything, many buildings were demolished and others damaged beyond repair, so they say. It's significant whether things in the area happened before '38 or after it.'

'Mrs Walcott loves to tell how her mother-in-law's piano ended up halfway across the street, and if you happened to be away from home you just took shelter where you could, I believe. It must have been terrifying. Do hurricanes come this way often?'

Oliver laughed. 'Bad storms sometimes, but nothing that compares with '38.' He led the way along the passage and opened a door which Veronica hadn't noticed previously. 'Take care, the stairs are fairly steep,' he said, offering his hand, which she took willingly. He kept it firmly in his own even when they reached the basement floor, and Veronica gasped at what she saw. 'A gym?' she exclaimed. 'So this is how you keep so fit?'

'I do my best—and—' he whispered, drawing her closer to his side, 'this is where I bring pretty girls to seduce them.'

She smiled up at him, responding to his nonsense. 'As long as you throw them out afterwards,' she said.

'You'd prefer that to being kept in chains in my dungeon?' he quipped, then pulled her behind him, pointing out the various pieces of equipment. 'Have a go on the exercise bicycle if you like, or the rowing machine. I won't suggest weights, that's a masculine pursuit, though I know some fitness classes persuade women to exercise with them, but I like women to be feminine. I might get hurt if one of my women develops their muscles too much!' He pinched her bare arm, saying: 'You're just right as you are, darling.'

Veronica sensed that his tone was becoming more intimate and she experienced butterflies in her stomach. She hadn't reckoned on being classed as 'one of his women', let alone being entertained at his luxury home.

'Then there's a sauna and a jacuzzi,' Oliver added, 'now I'm sure you'd enjoy that.'

'Yes, I love a sauna, but it's a bit warm today. I must confess I've never been in a jacuzzi.'

'You're too young to suffer from rheumatics yet, but I

believe the action of the water is very soothing to tired muscles, and we've been on the go since nine o'clock this morning, so how about it?'

The sauna was a decent size, accommodating about six people comfortably, but as Oliver explained, it would need time to heat up, while the jacuzzi was already filled and needed only to be switched on.

'It looks inviting,' Veronica agreed, 'but——'

'I know, the inevitable swimming costume. Um— well, there's only the two of us, and you don't seem too inhibited to me, do you really need one? I mean, the bubbling water will cover all your confusion, and I'll let you go in first, then switch on before I join you—and of course I'll get out and leave you to dress in privacy. I can't say fairer than that, can I?'

Veronica hesitated. Could she trust him? What kind of games was he used to playing? she wondered, and as if he could read her thoughts he asked: 'Don't you trust me? Veronica darling, I'm disappointed in you. I thought you knew me well enough to know that you're safe enough in my care.'

At once she rallied to reply. 'It's not that, Oliver. I'm just a bit apprehensive, that's all.'

'That's settled, then—off you go, have a quick shower, then into the pool, and as soon as I'm ready I'll switch on and be with you.' He took her through a doorway into a cosy area where there was a changing room and shower cubicle. After pushing a large bath sheet into her arms he left her, and there was little she could do but take all her clothes off and do as he had suggested. She emerged from the changing room with the bath sheet covering her from her armpits to her feet, and gently stepped down into the jacuzzi pool, carefully placing her feet on the steps until she was submerged and could sit on one of the side seats, leaving the towel on the floor at the side. A few minutes later she heard a door swing on its hinges and saw Oliver in swimming trunks come from the other changing room opposite the one she had used. He went to a switch on the wall and the water started to move. Veronica screamed with delight as her body seemed to lift off the seat, the hydro-massage gently stimulating her where the air jets forced the water to bubble beneath and around her. She was too busy concentrating on getting used to the unusual sensation to notice Oliver getting in beside her, but when she did she felt her skin tingle at the sight of his lean, wiry torso just above water level. She was thankful she was shorter than he so that more of her nakedness was submerged beneath the bubbling water.

'How does that feel?' Oliver asked. 'Invigorating, isn't it?'

'Different—but quite pleasant.' She glanced across at him, knowing that his intentions were not strictly honourable, no matter what he tried to pretend. It might all be innocent fun, but she knew she would be disappointed if Oliver didn't make some advances now, and wasn't this jacuzzi just the thing for making her pulses race, and if it was doing this to her what must his reactions be? She wasn't surprised therefore when she felt his big toe probing her dainty feet. He managed to find the sole of her left one, which nearly caused her to lose balance.

His eyes were darker blue now in the soft pinkish artificial light, full of mischievous intent and devilishly cunning as he teased her. 'You can swim, I take it?'

'Yes, or I wouldn't have accepted your generous offer,' she replied tersely.

'It wouldn't matter if you couldn't,' he said. 'It's not very deep, just like a rather large hexagonal-shaped bath.' He stood up to show her that the water barely came up to his waistline, a slim waistline with even slimmer hips just visible. He came over to her side of the pool and she was conscious of the broad shoulders as he placed his protecting arm around her, as well as the mat of coarse dark hair which covered his chest, and as he pulled her against him she felt the pressure of his prominent nipples against her skin. 'Losing your shyness?' he said, 'though I don't rate women's shyness very highly. It's all a pretence, isn't it, Veronica?'

'I . . . I am shy,' she confessed, 'when people force me

into situations I'm not prepared for.'

'So you weren't prepared for this? No one told you about my hideaway?'

'No—only that you had a bungalow somewhere, and I never expected to see it—after all, you don't normally get involved with members of the staff.'

'Aren't I involved with you already? Isn't there that chemical something that draws us together like a magnet, my darling Veronica?' Before she could deny it he had moved in closer, attaching his lips very firmly over hers until she felt herself forced backwards so that she lost her grip on the rail at the side of the pool, and found she was slipping down beneath him in the bubbling water. He held her fast, his lips never relaxing from the frenzied kiss even as he lifted her above water level and they were standing bodies pressed together until she could feel the heat of his desire. She tried to wriggle free; horseplay was one thing, but for heaven's sake, she didn't have anything on and she felt at a disadvantage. Oliver's modesty was intact as he was wearing swimming trunks.

He caught a fold of skin in her neck between his teeth, then finding a sensitive spot just below her ear rendered her helpless so that he could turn her round. He cradled her back into the contours of his own body, and such was the effect of his paralysing kiss that she went limp in his embrace. His hand went up to cup one of her breasts, while the other explored lower and more intimately until she was breathless. She was hardly aware of what she was doing, except that the feel of his damp skin beneath her fingers as she smoothed his thighs in response to his ardent persuasion only made her float away into the forbidden land of Eros. The gentle caress as his thumb manipulated her nipple until it was hard caused her to moan with pleasure—a pleasure she had never experienced before and wanted to continue for ever. Suddenly, as if some impulse had seized him, Oliver swept her up in his arms and carried her to the shower cubicle, where the kissing and caressing continued under the running warm water. He kept her facing towards him while he devoured every inch of her body.

'I knew it would be like this,' he muttered, arching his pelvis towards hers, and the touch of his skin against hers aroused her senses until she could hardly bear it.

'This is crazy, Oliver,' she breathed. 'We can't, we mustn't, it's too . . .' He silenced her with his tongue, sending fiery flames halfway down her throat so that she was speechless, and just when she thought she couldn't hold back the ecstasy any longer he reached up and turned the water off. She found herself wrapped in the huge sheet again, and as he pulled her behind him she noticed that he had put on a towelling robe. Back up the steps and into the master bedroom, where he began the compelling procedure all over again . . .

CHAPTER EIGHT

VERONICA stirred at some intrusion. She reached out for her lover, only to find that he had gone. He'd be back, she felt sure of that, and as she turned over on to her other side she relived the past few hours. First the jacuzzi and shower, and then the first delicious moment of complete fulfilment. Her body responded immediately to the memory which she would go on treasuring no matter what happened in the future. When they had returned to some degree of normality after what had seemed unrepeatable bliss, Oliver had insisted on a sauna, where desire was quickly aroused yet again, and Veronica had reached heights of rapture she never thought possible, and then they had lain together on this couchette in the basement. Sleep had come on wings of satisfaction; how long had she been here? She rolled over and held her arm up to look at her watch. Only seven o'clock. She felt as if she had been here at the bungalow for at least twenty-four hours. But where was Oliver? She lifted herself up and listened—yes, she could hear his voice in the distance, he must be on the phone, and as reality crept back to replace the insanity of earlier she realised that it was the telephone bell which had roused her.

It was very warm down in the basement and they had shared the couchette naked and in complete harmony, but now Veronica began to have doubts about her willingness to share Oliver's body. He was known not to get involved with hospital staff, so how much value did he place on the past few hours of lovemaking? She was totally committed to him and she knew there could never be anyone else now. But surely, she told herself, such passion must mean that he had committed himself to her too? Yet deep inside she knew there was uncertainty, and fear along with guilt-ridden apprehension made her get off the couchette and get dressed. She was just putting on her sandals when she heard Oliver's light tread coming down the cellar steps. 'Ah, so you've come back to me at last!' he smiled.

'Was it the phone that woke us?' she asked, hardly daring to look directly at him.

Oliver was wearing his towelling robe and he came to stand before her, eyes sleepily provocative. 'I didn't want you to dress just yet—but perhaps it's as well you did, I'm afraid I've had an urgent call back to Brookville. There's time for a cup of tea, though, so while I dress would you do the honours, please, darling?'

'Of course—and I think it was high time I got dressed,' she said decisively.

He chuckled as he held her elbows gently in his hands—hands which had shown her how easily she could be tempted into submission. 'Not feeling guilty, are you?' he questioned lightheartedly.

Veronica shook her head and without a smile said: 'I know I should be. I don't like casual affairs, I've never indulged before.'

'But you have had boyfriends before, you can't deny that?'

'I haven't denied it, but I was young and thought I was in love, but then his career meant more to him than a wife and I soon became involved with having to look after my mother—the rest you know.'

'The man must have been a fool,' Oliver remarked drily. 'Not only are you attractive with the kind of body any man would love to possess, but you make such sweet music, my dear Veronica.'

With a coy smile at him she said: 'You're not so bad at it yourself.'

He inclined his head with a generous, warm smile. 'I'd better get dressed, or I might forget that telephone call!'

He wasn't likely to do that, Veronica realised. However much a woman charmed him he would always keep his priorities in the right order, and devotion to duty was top of his list. She should count herself fortunate that she had managed to claim his attention for this many hours, helping him to forget he was a workaholic and sharing such intimacy with him. In his country kitchen she rinsed out the mugs and teapot and waited for the kettle to boil, her doubts increasing. She was a fool, she told herself, just because she felt the way she did about him there was no reason to forget her strict principles and grab what precious moments of happiness she could, regardless of his feelings for her. Was it possible that he had forgotten Maud long enough to realise that he was capable of loving another woman? As much as Maud, though? No, it would have to be more to satisfy Veronica's demands. There were to be no half measures in her love-life. She loved Oliver with utter and complete honesty, but had he used her merely to satisfy his sexual urges? She rather thought he had, and she felt disappointed, as much with herself as with him.

When he came into the kitchen he was dressed in a lightweight suit with fashionable tie and matching shirt. Her heart swelled with love for him all over again, and she refused to deny herself the warmth of his embrace as he came to stand beside her, his hand encircling her waist.

'You won't mind being back this early, will you? We had an early start this morning, so I daresay you have things to do to get ready for work tomorrow?'

'Yes, I can always write letters,' she said, though fully aware that her mind was too confused for any such activity. 'I hope it's nothing too drastic that you've been called out for? It's a good job we were back, isn't it?'

She felt the pressure of his fingers which excited her as he laughed. 'Just as well the call didn't come any earlier—I'm not at all sure I could have handled it,' he said.

On impulse she answered, 'I'm sure you would have done admirably. Work always comes first with you, doesn't it?'

'I see,' he said, with a touch of complaint in his voice. 'You think that while I was making love to you I was in the operating theatre in my mind? For heaven's sake,

Veronica, what sort of callous beast do you think I am? Was I that mechanical about it? Maybe I was too over the top to notice, but I could have sworn you were up in the clouds with me.'

'Oliver,' she implored, 'you know I was completely out of this world, you were wonderful! I didn't mean that.'

'Then what the hell were you implying? That I can be that good and still have time to consider Brookville, or does Brookville have to compete with you—ah! I understand, I think. Like all women it has to be all or nothing—total commitment to you?'

'You're a doctor, I know the score,' she said. 'I can't hope to compete.'

She made the tea and he moved away from her side. She had wounded him, she realised, and that wasn't what she had intended, but she had probably touched on the truth, and that in turn hurt her pride.

Oliver left her to drink her tea alone, and when he did return to the lounge it was obvious that he was anxious to be off, so in a matter of minutes they were driving through the leafy lane and heading for Groton, but he stopped off at Riverside to let her out.

'Thanks for a lovely day, Oliver,' Veronica said in a husky but genuinely grateful tone.

He bent to kiss her as she got out of the car. 'I'm glad you enjoyed it,' he said, but there was an edge to his tone and no mention of further dates.

Veronica watched him go, and tears began to gather behind her eyes. Why couldn't she keep her mouth shut? She'd had a fantastic time and now she'd messed it up by making snide remarks about Oliver being dedicated to his work, something which she admired him for in truth. She was glad she got upstairs without meeting anyone, and she hoped desperately that no one would come seeking her company this evening, though that was unlikely as secrets were hard to keep in a hospital, wherever in the world it might be situated, and by now everyone would know that she had been out with Oliver today.

She realised after a while that she was quite hungry, so she made an omelette and was enjoying some coffee in her small lounge when the telephone rang. She jumped up. Could it be Oliver? Perhaps he wasn't needed after all, but a strange female voice spoke. 'Is that Miss Summers?' Veronica said it was. 'My name is Margaret Hughes, I was Margaret Duvall, so you'll know that I'm calling on behalf of my father, Burt Duvall, who I believe you're anxious to trace?'

'Oh!' Veronica could hardly believe her ears. 'My letter found him? I'm so pleased,' she said, her excitement mounting. 'How is he? There's so much I want to know.'

'This is just a brief call, Miss Summers, to say that if you can get over to Rochester we'll be happy to see you.'

Something softened Veronica's enthusiasm, and she spoke more slowly. 'That would be really nice,' she said. 'But I don't want to inconvenience anyone. I've explained that my mother is dead now, but she asked me to try to find him if I ever came to the States. Is there anywhere close to you where I can stay—a motel or hotel perhaps?'

'Yes, there's a Howard Johnson's right close to the airport. If you let us know when you're coming I can be there to meet you and see you settled in.'

'As you know I'm working at Brookville hospital here, so I'll have to make the necessary arrangements first,' said Veronica. 'I've been saving up my days off so that I'd have plenty of free time to visit Mr Duvall if I ever found him. I can't tell you how thrilled I am that you've called. It's so kind of you. Perhaps I could have your phone number so that I can call you when I've made arrangements?'

The voice at the other end recited a code and number in Rochester, then Veronica was left still holding the receiver, not really certain quite what she had let herself in for. She tried to tell herself that the voice on the other end hadn't been any more distant than the miles necessitated, that Margaret Hughes had been friendly, and that her mother's dying wish was to be granted. Veronica couldn't sleep. She tossed and turned, sometimes reliving her moments of passion with Oliver, and then as she dozed fitfully she was flying off somewhere or running, running, yet no one seemed to be chasing her. She wished Oliver had contacted her again so that she could tell him the good news, but he was evidently otherwise occupied and she must be content to wait until morning. She was glad when her alarm sounded and she could get up. She had made up her mind to see Oliver and ask to have the time due to her as soon as possible, like today or tomorrow. Once she was in Rochester she could take her time in making arrangements to see her grandfather, and now that it looked like becoming a reality she felt nervous, yet still determined.

She was so anxious to share her news with Oliver that she drove carelessly and was pulled over by the traffic police, but once they realised she was one of Brookville's nurses and on her way to work, they were overwhelmingly polite, and allowed her to continue with a caution. When she reached the hospital she dashed inside to Oliver's office, but he wasn't there, so she located Natalie behind her desk.

'Ah, Natalie,' she said in a rush. 'Any idea where Oliver is?'

Natalie grinned, and Veronica took it to mean that she knew that they had spent the day together yesterday, but the head nurse replied: 'Yes, Veronica, down in Orlando.'

'*Orlando!*' The echo leapt from Veronica's astonished lips. She felt the colour drain from her cheeks as she stared stupidly at Natalie.

'My dear, is anything wrong?'

Veronica blinked. 'No, no,' she said more calmly. 'It's just that I've heard from the people in Rochester, so I really wanted to take my holiday as soon as possible.'

'Gosh! That's marvellous, Veronica. Of course you'll want to leave right away.'

'Well, Oliver did say not to do anything without consulting him first,' Veronica explained.

'I'll OK it with him. Of course you must take the time

due to you. Do you need any help with flights and things? Oh, I'm so excited for you, I'll help with anything, anything!'

It seemed that Veronica was swept along on a tide of enthusiasm not entirely of her own volition. Dave was brought into the scene, and took her himself into the travel agency to collect her ticket which Natalie had booked by phone.

'Dave, I don't really like going off without telling Oliver,' she said worriedly as they drove back to Brookville. 'Does he ring in or anything? Any idea how long he'll be gone?'

'None at all, and he may or may not get in touch. Depends what he and Maud are up to. I know you and he spent the day together yesterday, but for goodness' sake don't read too much into it. OK, so he doesn't agree with what you're doing, but it's your life and it has to be your decision. I'll make sure he understands that your folks in Rochester invited you there, that way he can't complain, can he?'

'But he did say not to go without his knowledge,' Veronica replied loyally.

'He won't remember that once he's been with Maud for a while. You go off while you've got the chance, and good luck.'

But Veronica was not entirely happy when the time came for her to leave. Dave drove her the short distance to the airport and watched her off on the small Pilgrim aircraft with its significant green and orange markings. She'd never get used to a plane this size, she thought as it taxied down the runway, but it was soon up and circling, and looking down she could see Dave clearly on the ground waving in her direction.

Both Natalie and Dave had given her clear instructions as to which terminal at Kennedy she needed to catch the flight to Rochester, which she did without any trouble. She could hardly believe it when she took off again and in just an hour was landing at Rochester airport. Margaret Hughes had assured that she would be there waiting for her, and that she would be recognisable

by her ash-blonde hair and green trouser-suit. It was a
smallish airport with few preliminaries to deal with, so
before she knew it Veronica was shaking hands with a
nicely rounded woman in her mid-thirties, she thought.

'We're so pleased you could come,' Margaret Hughes
drawled in her soft American accent, but Veronica
sensed that there was some restraint in her manner.

'It's very good of you to give up your time to meet me,'
said Veronica. 'I suppose I could hire a car to get
around. I certainly don't intend to be a burden on you.'

'You won't be that, Veronica. Pa's looking forward to
meeting you, so I guess we'll go straight home to please
him, then we'll see you safely to Howard Johnson's
later. I'm only sorry we don't have room for you to stay
with us—I hope you understand.'

'It's quite all right. Howard Johnsons come in useful. I
was obliged to stay in one at Kennedy when I first
arrived.' Veronica followed Margaret Hughes out to a
waiting car and they drove through streets much like any
other town in any other country. Margaret pulled up at a
smart little house in a tree-lined avenue, and almost at
once an elderly man came through the front door. He
was white-haired, tall and erect for his age, with
sparkling blue eyes and a fresh complexion.

'Well, well, well,' he greeted, 'if it isn't like seeing
young Betty all over again!' He hugged Veronica and
kissed her while Margaret put the car in the driveway, a
shared one with their next-door neighbour. 'I hope
you've brought me some photographs, young lady, of
my Betty. You know, I can hardly believe she's gone on
before me. I know I'm not so young at seventy-two, but
Betty was five years younger. But come along in, we've a
lot to talk about.'

It was a pleasant little house where Burt lived with his
daughter and her husband, Andrew. They apologised
profusely for not being able to accommodate her with
them, but Veronica assured them several times that she
was quite happy to stay a short distance down the road.
She was surprised to find how humid it was in Rochester
and was glad of a drink of fresh orange juice before they

sat down to dinner. She wasn't quite sure how to broach the subject of who she was, yet it seemed apparent that they knew she was related to Betty Smith. 'I wasn't sure whether I was doing the right thing by trying to contact you, Mr Duvall,' she said.

'Now you just call me Pa or Burt like everyone else, Veronica,' he smiled. 'The war's been over a long time, but I reckon young Betty and me would have loved each other wherever we were or however long we lived. I'm only sorry she wouldn't come to the States.'

'Do you know why she wouldn't!' Veronica asked.

'Why, the baby, of course. Your mother.'

'You knew she had a baby?' Veronica exclaimed.

'Not for some years after I'd married. My old buddy went to England for a holiday and he looked young Betty up, and there she was, pretty as a picture with this child nearly as pretty as herself. T'was too late to turn the clock back then . . .'

Veronica felt choked for him. He was obviously distressed, and the advice she had been given not to rake up the past hammered in her brain, and she knew she shouldn't have meddled in affairs which didn't directly concern her, and which time had made impossible to change.

'I shouldn't have come . . .' she began.

'And deprive an old man of seeing his granddaughter?'

'There's no need to be on guard, Veronica,' Margaret said kindly. 'Pa's told us the story many times. There's no love like an old love, so they say. Ma never held it against him, she just wished they'd all met up before your mother and grandmother died. What we can't make out is why your mother waited so long to contact Pa.'

'She didn't tell us that she'd found your letters—Burt,' Veronica explained. 'We knew that Gran had our mother, Rosalie, illegitimately, and by an American soldier, but that was all. Gran and Mum made a happy life together even if they didn't have much money, and when Mum met Dad, although they were very young, they got married, and Gran always stayed with them. We were a very happy and united family until first Gran died and then Mum.'

After the meal was finished Veronica helped Margaret with the dishes while Burt had his customary nap. It gave the women time to get to know each other, and Veronica was just beginning to feel less awkward when Margaret's husband Andrew returned from work. He was a very large man who worked in a factory close by, and although he greeted Veronica cordially enough it was obvious that he was suspicious of her.

'So,' he said in a too loud voice, 'what's brought you three thousand miles across the Atlantic? Searching for gold?' He laughed heartily, but Veronica recognised some sarcasm behind his question.

'It was my mother's wish that I should try to find her father,' she said in her most efficient nurse's tone. 'I have to admit I wasn't particularly keen to do so, but once I'd arrived in America to work I knew I had to do as she asked.'

'So? You've found him—what now?'

'Pa's glad to have heard first-hand news of the girl he left behind in England,' Margaret put in.

'Sure am,' a voice said from the lounge doorway. 'And I mean to keep her here until I've heard all the news, about the woman who should have been my wife; and my baby girl. It's just great to see the granddaughter I never knew existed until a while ago, and in case you need proof that I knew and loved Betty Smith, here's the picture I've carried around with me for over forty years.' He held out a faded photograph of a girl very similar to how Veronica looked now. 'Twenty-three she was then—in 1943, and then we had a war to finish. It took time to get back to normal after that, you know. You youngsters don't know what it was like.'

'Come on, Pa, what about Vietnam? That was no picnic either.'

'No, Andy, you're right there. War of any kind ain't no picnic. There were plenty of girls left like poor Betty, but I'd have got back to England if I'd known. Feel bad about that, I do. She should have told me, but I reckon she didn't want me to marry her just on account of the baby. But there was more to it than that. She knew I loved her—I wrote often enough to tell her, but it's my belief that she thought t'would bring disgrace on my family. I guess they'd have been pretty shook up about it at that, but I'd have stood by her and we'd have managed somehow.'

'Pa, why don't you take Veronica for a little walk in the garden or down the road a block or two while I get tea and Andy gets washed up?' suggested Margaret.

Burt agreed, and Veronica was quite relieved to get out of the house for a while. She tucked her arm through Burt's as they sauntered down the road while he talked about the war, and Veronica told him as much as she could remember of her grandmother. It wasn't difficult to give him a graphic picture of his daughter, her mother, and she knew it pleased him to hear all about the child he had never known.

Conversation wasn't so easy back at the house where she felt that Andy was decidedly antagonistic towards her, but it wasn't until he said: 'All Pa's got is his pension, you know,' that she realised he must think she had come to see if she could claim some inheritance or other. She felt sick inside, and wished she had done as Oliver had suggested and left well alone. She had seen her grandfather and could understand why her grand-mother had loved him so singlemindedly, but now she would go back to Groton and try to concentrate on the remaining weeks and months of her year-long work agreement at Brookville.

Later Margaret drove her to the hotel and insisted on seeing that the room was suitable, and that Veronica had everything she required.

'I shall only be staying a day or two,' Veronica told her, hoping that this would quell any ideas they had about her money-grubbing. 'I'm here on a work permit, so I have to get back to Groton.'

Margaret slumped down on the bed. 'But I thought

you said you had some holiday due to you? Pa's expecting you to stay much longer than a few days, Veronica.'

'Then I'm sorry if I misled him.'

'If it's too expensive to stay here then you can always have a bed made up on the couch in the lounge,' Margaret insisted. 'Veronica, you can't come into Pa's life like a dream and walk out of it again so soon! He's set his heart on showing you Niagara Falls and other beauty spots.'

Veronica laughed vaguely. 'But that isn't up to Burt, is it? It means you've got to be bothered with me, and I can understand that you don't want an intruder.'

Margaret banged her forehead with her fist. 'I get it—you've taken offence at my Andy. Well, I must admit we both wondered what you might be after, and we did try to put Pa off, which is why you didn't get a quick reply to your letter, but it upset him so much that I knew I had to let you come, and now that I've met you—well, *I* want you to stay. It'll be like a holiday for me too. Maybe I can persuade Andy to take the odd day off to help with the driving. Honestly, Veronica, I'm real sorry if he seemed offish with you. It's just his way, and he was worried for Pa and me. Ma would have loved you, though. You'd have thought she'd have been jealous of this woman, Betty, who was always in Pa's mind, but I guess she learned to love her just as much as he did, and when he learned that he had a daughter— just think of it, Veronica, your Ma and me, we'd have been half-sisters.'

Veronica stared at her for a few minutes, then they both laughed. 'So that makes you my aunt—or half-aunt,' she said. 'Isn't life complicated?'

'I guess so, but seriously, Veronica, isn't there some way you can ask for more time? I know you can always come back, but Pa's going to be real disappointed if you only stay for a couple of days. I'm sorry if you thought we were a bit wary—but you never know about folks, do you? We don't have any doubts now, though. According to Pa you're just like your grandmother, and we do want

to get to know you better. I know we said that we
couldn't put you up—it was better that way until we'd
actually met you. You do understand, don't you?'

'Indeed I do, Margaret,' Veronica answered, 'and
thanks for the offer of staying with you, but it's best if I
stay put here. For one thing, I feel this must be putting a
strain on you all, but mostly Burt. He's not a young man
and he needs time to get used to the idea.'

'He's pretty tough. He's had the usual prostate problems, and he doesn't realise how serious it is, but his
heart isn't as good as it was. Andy's been great in having
Pa come to live with us. It's never an easy decision to
make, having elderly parents to live with you, it can put a
dreadful strain on a marriage, but he and Ma were so
wonderful to us when—we lost our baby.' Margaret
gulped and struggled against the tide of emotion which
had caught her unawares. 'I . . . I'm sorry, you must
think I'm silly. It was seven years ago, I should be over it
by now.'

Veronica sat down on the bed beside Margaret and
put her arm round her shoulders. 'I do understand. Life
can be cruel, and I doubt that you'll ever get over it. It
just doesn't go away, does it? I still feel emotional about
losing my mother—she was so young, only forty-one,
not much older than you, I suppose.'

'I'm thirty-six, and I'd have loved to give my parents a
grandchild, but now Burt has you, and that's made him
so happy.'

'But can't you have any more children, Margaret?'

'At first I didn't want to know. I might have felt
differently if Holly had died at birth, but we had her for
seven months and it was agony to lose her, especially as
we thought she was only suffering from a snuffly cold.
Well, you're a nurse, so I don't have to tell you that these
inexplicable deaths happen. It broke Ma's heart, and
within eighteen months she'd gone too. So you see, for a
long while I couldn't even contemplate having another
baby, but now——' Margaret got up and walked to the
window looking down on the world far below the
twentieth storey. 'I long to hold another child in my

arms. It's become an obsession, Veronica—help me! What can I do? And don't suggest adoption—I want my own baby!'

Veronica chose her words with care. 'We can't alter what fate decides for us, Margaret. Maybe, though, you're trying too hard, thinking about it too much, dwelling on it when you should be getting on with your life as it is. Do you work?'

'No. Andy won't let me, he says I have enough to do to look after Pa and him, and he's right. I'm not complaining. Pa and me get on like a house on fire, and we live very comfortably. I have interests too, like sewing and reading.'

'Perhaps you need to get out more,' Veronica suggested. 'What about voluntary work—helping with homeless people or orphaned children?'

'That's what my doctor suggested at the time, but I wasn't ready to do anything like that then. I suppose I could be more use to the community now. I'll have to see what Andy thinks.'

Veronica didn't say any more. No doubt Andy would immediately think it was Veronica who had been putting ideas into his wife's head. 'Shall I ring down for some coffee or something?' she offered instead.

Margaret pulled her bag up over her shoulder. 'No, thanks. I must get on, though I hate leaving you here alone like this.'

Veronica laughed it off. 'It's OK, honestly. I'm used to being alone quite a bit.'

Reluctantly Margaret left the hotel, and Veronica had to admit to herself that she felt dreadfully isolated. After such a superb day spent with Oliver, and then the busy time yesterday making all the arrangements, the excitement of travelling and meeting Burt and his family today, the loneliness came as an anticlimax, leaving her feeling desolate. She unpacked her few personal belongings, then took a long leisurely bath which gave her time to reflect . . .

Oliver had very cleverly snared her into his net of escapism, and she, fool that she was, had given herself to him unconditionally. She felt anger swelling inside her, anger that he had used her for his own satisfaction which evidently had merely given him a more lusty appetite to go after the woman he really loved. She should have thought, she should have known he wasn't capable of loving anyone else except Maud. Now she had cheapened herself in his eyes, and he probably didn't care a jot about her feelings, or that she had come rushing off to Rochester. There was only one thing to do, and that was to forget him as quickly as she could, though it was going to be the hardest thing she had ever had to undertake.

She loved him to distraction, even though she was desperately trying to tell herself that any man who could take what he wanted so glibly wasn't worth it. She wished she could hate him, she did for treating her so casually, but deep inside her, right at the core of her heart, she knew that a love had grown which was like no other. She had heard about and met women who loved men who treated them badly, knocked them around, called them names, despised them, and yet a deep, unquestionable love still remained. She had declared that such women were slaves—now she herself was a slave to Oliver. If he came making demands at this minute she would ingratiate herself, submit willingly in the cause of her underlying passion for the man.

The water was sensuously warm, soon it would go cold, but her thoughts and memories of the masterful way he had manipulated her kept her blood at maximum temperature. True love shouldn't be like this, she thought, it didn't need to be so painful, but if you were silly enough to fall in love with the wrong man—and not for the first time, she reminded herself with a touch of shame—you must bear the anguish without complaint. It was a new experience to love this much, she argued. Before, she had been young, Terry had been young and they had been swept away on a tempestuous wave of what they thought was genuine love, but which, in fact, had been puppy love. All too rapidly they had grown out of their need for one another, and now he was somewhere on the other side of the world in New Zealand, married to a Maori girl who bore him a child each year. It had taken Veronica a long while to get over Terry; was it going to be another five years to get Oliver out of her system? She felt that having shared their love they had made a blood bond between them. Had it meant so little to him? Life was certainly cruel, she reasserted, and with a whoosh she got up out of the tub and dried herself with condemning aggression.

She didn't sleep right through the night. Strange noises disturbed her, and when the first plane took off at the nearby airport about five a.m. she was already awake and wishing she could rush to catch it. Oliver had been right about the stupidity of making wild goose chases, but after breakfast later, when to her surprise Margaret and Burt walked into the hotel, she forgot her misgivings and greeted them warmly.

'Pa just had to come to check that you're all right,' Margaret told her. 'He doesn't trust hotels, and he couldn't leave it to me to come and fetch you. I wondered if you'd be sleeping in this morning.'

'I'm usually an early bird,' Veronica said. 'And in spite of the air-conditioning it's rather warm in my room.'

'The humidity does take some getting used to,' said Burt. 'But you'll soon adapt, and what's this I hear about you only staying for a couple of days? Nonsense! Let me talk to your boss, I'll soon set him straight.'

'That's fighting talk, Burt,' Veronica said with a laugh, and wondered just what Oliver would make of her distant relatives. Yes, they were all branches of the same family tree. Burt was her grandfather, and she felt the affinity with him while talking so lovingly of her grandmother and mother, which brought them all a lot closer, and made her glow with a new inner awareness of family ties.

She took Burt and Margaret up to her room so that he could confirm that it was satisfactory, and when she had cleaned her teeth they went down in the lift and out to the car. They agreed on a fairly quiet day, though it was obvious that a great deal of discussion had taken place in her absence and some exciting plans made. After lunch while Burt was having his rest Margaret and Veronica sat on the front porch step in the shade and chatted amicably. The change in Margaret's manner was such that Veronica felt she had known the older girl all her life, and even Andy seemed more inclined to accept her when he returned from work in the early evening.

'I'm going to take a long weekend,' he announced, 'but I want to be sure you're going to stay that long, Veronica.'

'I ought to check with the hospital first, I suppose, but I'm due for a week at least. On the other hand, I don't want you to use up holiday which you might need later on, Andy.'

'Can you get in touch with anyone this evening? Call from here after supper, then I shall know what to arrange at work. I'm foreman on my floor, so I can please myself up to a point, but I like to make sure I'll be covered.'

Veronica fell fairly silent while the conversation washed over her. She wondered if Oliver was back, but he hadn't informed her of his movements, so why should she worry what he thought? She'd be almost sure to get Natalie at Brookville, and after supper the others left her alone in the lounge while she put through a call to Groton.

Natalie was quickly found and came on the line excitedly. 'Hi, Veronica, how are things? Is everything OK? Is your grandfather pleased to see you?'

Veronica laughed at her questioning. 'Everything's lovely,' she said, not wanting to go into the details of how she had felt at first. 'I know I've got a week due to me, so is it all right if I stay until next Tuesday?'

'Of course, no problem, have a good time while you can. We're all delighted for you.'

'Er . . . is . . . Oliver back yet?' she ventured to enquire.

'No, but don't worry about him. I'll tell him the news when he turns up, and he'll be pleased for you, I'm sure.'

The family were delighted that she could stay for the whole week, but no matter how much they tried to persuade her to move in with them, Veronica insisted that she remain at the hotel so that she wasn't putting them out. 'I'm not a pauper,' she laughed. 'Nurses are very well paid over here, and the hours are excellent. I won't say it's been like a holiday, we do work very hard when we are at work, but I'm really enjoying the experience, and I can afford a week away—honestly.'

'I feel bad about that, though,' said Burt. 'My own granddaughter—I want to pay for your stay at Howard Johnson's.'

'Now, Pa, you've only got your pension,' Andy reminded the old man.

'And I'll spend it any way I want to!'

Veronica held up her hands to quieten them. 'Please, Burt, it's all right, and if I run into debt I'll tell you —how's that?'

'Only you won't, because Andy's making it quite plain that he thinks you're after my money, and you're a Duvall, my girl, you've got the pride of my family all right. Well, you just have it your own way, but if I want to buy you a present, I shall.' The old man turned and shuffled away out into the small garden.

'Now look what you've done, Andy,' grumbled Margaret. 'He's upset, and I don't want him to be.'

'I'll talk to him,' Veronica offered, 'and then I must go if we're to have an early start tomorrow.'

In her own tactful way she calmed her grandfather, assuring him that it was right for Andy to be suspicious of her, but now that it was all out in the open the suspicion would soon fade.

Margaret drove her back to Howard Johnson's and Veronica was determined to get an early night and some much-needed sleep, in readiness for the trips which had been planned.

She watched television once she was in bed and soon became drowsy, so she switched it off and was nicely comfortable when the telephone roused her again. She picked the receiver up quickly, anticipating some change of plan, but a masculine voice shouted down the line in answer to her 'Hello'. 'What the hell do you think you're doing, dashing off to Rochester without my permission?' Oliver demanded.

Veronica couldn't find her voice immediately, so he went on: 'I made it quite clear that you weren't to leave Brookville without my knowledge—and staying in a hotel by yourself!'

Now Veronica was in a sitting position, her cheeks scarlet with rage. 'Shut up!' she snapped aggressively. 'You aren't my keeper, I'll do what I want to do. You were quite aware of the fact that I was waiting for a call or letter from my grandfather, so here I am and here I'm staying!' She slammed down the receiver and fumed.

Within thirty seconds the phone rang again. She stared at it, her heartbeats drumming in her ears, her throat dry with anger—pent-up anger at the way Oliver had deserted her, and then come back treating her like his property. It rang and rang—and she knew he wouldn't give up.

'Yes?' she said stonily.

'How dare you hang up on me, Veronica!' he snarled. 'I'm responsible for my staff, and phone calls from Florida cost money.'

So he was still in Orlando with his beloved Maud.

'How did you know I'd come to Rochester, then?' she asked icily.

'Because, my dear, I wanted to talk to you, and I was not at all pleased that you'd taken off without having the courtesy to tell me.'

'Oliver,' she said in a sickly-sweet voice, 'you didn't consider it necessary to keep me informed of your whereabouts. I had no idea until I asked where you were that you'd gone down to Orlando.'

'Oh yes, you did,' he argued. 'I told you that phone call was from Maud and that I had to leave at once.'

She drew herself up and her intake of indignant breath must have been audible from Rochester to Orlando. 'You . . . you—liar!' she screamed at him. 'I was asleep at the time . . .' She wished she hadn't said that. She didn't want to be reminded of that eventful afternoon and she was quite sure that Oliver didn't want to be reminded of it either.

The line seemed to have gone dead. Veronica held the receiver away from her ear and stared at it, her cheeks stiff with apprehension. Had he hung up on her?

'Yes,' he crooned more softly now, 'I do remember, which is why I suppose I didn't think to mention who'd called.' There seemed to be a long, conciliatory pause. Too long, during which Veronica calmed considerably, and evidently so did Oliver. 'So you've found your family? Are they all right?' he enquired.

'Yes, thank you.' She was being much more terse than she wanted to be. She would so much rather have come right out with the truth, that she loved him and wanted him, far more than she needed her new family.

'Are you happy now?' he asked. 'Are they happy?'

'I'm very glad I came. Grandfather's a dear, and his daughter too. Her husband was a bit suspicious of me to begin with, it seems he thought I'd come all this way to steal the family silver.'

'The *what!*' echoed Oliver.

'Well, an inheritance or anything that was going, which is why I'm staying right here at the hotel. It's very comfortable, and it gives me time to think.'

'So everything is not all right, Veronica,' Oliver stated. 'I did warn you that they might not take kindly to an unknown relative turning up on their doorstep.'

'I didn't mean that,' she replied with a half-hearted laugh.

'Let me know what time you expect to be back and I'll see that you're met,' he replied shortly.

Pride wouldn't allow Veronica to ask how much longer he would be staying in Orlando, so she thanked him politely and the telephone conversation came to an end. She noted that he hadn't said he would meet her himself. She sat up in bed after replacing the receiver and breathed a sigh of relief—at least the worry of him not knowing that she had come to Rochester was over, though why he was so angry she couldn't imagine. She wasn't taking extra time off, the week was due to her and probably a few days more, and she might even be persuaded to stay longer, she decided defiantly.

CHAPTER NINE

THE WEATHER was splendid, and Veronica's new-found family did everything they could to make her stay enjoyable. She telephoned home to England and in turn they all spoke with her father and Ellie. There was so much catching up to do that Veronica and Burt spent many happy hours just chatting. She learned that he had been injured during the latter part of the war and returned to the States where he was hospitalised for several months. His family had been against him trying to contact Betty Smith, so their correspondence had been secret and through his friend.

'She broke my heart,' he said, 'when she ignored my letters as time went by. I only knew about your mother through a chance meeting when my buddy and his wife came back from a holiday in England some years later, and he told me he'd called to see Betty. I toyed with the idea of making a similar trip, but my wife didn't enjoy the best of health and didn't care to travel, then she got sick, so it was out of the question. By then I was left with fading memories of Betty, though I was real upset to hear that she never married, but it was too late for me to make amends, and besides, my duty was with my folks here. I guess poor Betty had as much as she could manage to provide for herself and the child. I only wish she'd told me about her right after the war.'

'My grandmother was a proud woman, Burt,' Veronica told him. 'She lived and worked for herself and her daughter, determined not to take charity from anyone.'

'But it wouldn't have been charity—t'was my duty to provide for them, and I would have if she'd told me the truth. I guess she didn't understand that when I was injured and came back here our lives were pretty much upside down. Then again, when she knew that I'd been wounded she kept quiet about the baby because she

155

didn't want to worry me.'

'That was Gran,' Veronica said, with admiration in her voice, and Burt reached out and squeezed her hand. 'She didn't let on to anyone that she ever heard from you, much less say that you wanted her to come to America. Mum certainly never knew that. Poor Gran, to think she lived with her secrets for so long! If only we'd known more details we could have been kinder about it all.'

'That's the way of the world, Veronica,' Burt said gently. 'We all pre-judge other folk without knowing the full facts—and I guess we have to make allowances for the main fact, which is that the world was in a hell of a mess when the war ended.'

Burt fell into a thoughtful silence. They were on their way to Niagara Falls. Andy had taken the day off to drive them, so Veronica and her grandfather were sitting together in the back of the car. It was a beautiful day and Veronica was a little more acclimatised to the humidity now, realising that wearing the minimum of clothes was the best way to dress. The road was wide all along the route, and they passed through pretty villages until at last they reached the bridge which was the border between Canada and America. Veronica felt quite excited.

'When I was at school I did a project about Canada,' she told them, 'and I've always longed to see Niagara Falls, but I never expected to be able to.'

'You'll sure get your fill of it today,' Andy said. 'Believe me, we never tire of visiting it either.'

After they had crossed the bridge into Canada, Veronica was required to go to the Customs Office, and then they proceeded along River Road to the tourist area at Horseshoe Falls, where Andy parked the car. The sound of rushing water was like music to Veronica's ears and she could hardly wait until she was standing by the rail with spray tickling her face.

'It's a magnificent sight!' she breathed, but when Andy suggested that she might like to take a boat trip to get a closer view of the Falls she declined his offer. 'It looks so treacherous,' she said. 'Look how the boat gets tossed about, and it goes so close to the rocks. Surely they must have dreadful accidents here?'

'Not with the boats, the pressure of the tumbling water keeps them back. There are accidents, and amazing rescues too. A few years ago a man was in a boat up there on the river with his two children. He didn't realise that he'd reached the rapids, the boat capsized and the children were caught in the current and tossed over the Falls. One child was seen and rescued by one of the boats, and she insisted that her brother was there somewhere, so the boat went in and searched until he was found, and they both survived—nothing short of a miracle.'

As it was almost lunchtime they went into the restaurant where they could sit and look out at the Falls while Veronica and Margaret enjoyed their weight-watcher's platter which consisted of chicken salad, followed by fruit, and the men had sole and chips. Veronica was determined to take her fill of this wonder of the world, and out in the sunshine once more they took a ride on the run-about trailer which went along the river's edge, where they had a better view of the rapids and an old barge which had been there for many years and which was impossible to salvage.

Burt was feeling quite tired, so he went to sit in the car to rest while Andy and Margaret took Veronica up in the cliff lift to the Panavision tower where she could obtain the best views.

'I wouldn't have missed this for the world,' she said excitedly. 'I've achieved my life-long ambition.'

'Guess you're pretty easy to please, then,' said Andy. 'Shouldn't you have an ambition to get married? That's usually what a girl of your age wants most, isn't it?'

'Andy!' Margaret reproached. 'Isn't that kinda personal?'

Veronica laughed. 'I haven't had too much time to think about that,' she said. 'My career has been important to me after caring for Mum and Dad, and worrying about Ellie. But—well, yes, I would like to be married.'

'Anyone in particular?' asked Margaret.

'Mm . . . there is a doctor I'm very fond of, but I'm

afraid he's already spoken for.'

'Tough luck. Here or at home?'

Veronica sighed. She needed to talk to someone, and wasn't Margaret like a sister? Besides, they were never likely to meet Oliver Linley here on the other side of New York State.

'At Brookville, where else?' she said dispassionately. 'I'll just have to make the most of it while I've got the chance, but he goes down to Orlando frequently, it seems.'

'You think he has a girlfriend down there?'

'Yes, she's a doctor that he's known for a very long time. He admitted to me that he once had the most enormous crush on her. He says he's over it, but I'm sure he's not, and in time they'll get together, I expect.'

'What's been stopping them up until now, then?'

'That's the puzzle. He tried to give the impression that there's nothing in it, but if you saw them together and the way they look at each other there isn't much doubt about how they feel. I suppose it could be something to do with the fact that she's foreign, Russian I think, or maybe she's married to someone else, although Oliver did say that her work is her life.'

'It's possible that their profession is enough in their lives,' Margaret said wisely, and Veronica let the matter drop. Maybe that was so for Maud, but not for Oliver. He was a dedicated doctor, there was no denying that, but he was also a virile man who needed a woman's affection, he had shown that clearly at his bungalow. But—she turned her memories over in her mind—he, like any other healthy man, needed to exercise his sexual passions, and that was all his afternoon with Veronica had meant. It had all ended abruptly, and she hated him for the way he had kept secret the fact that he was going straight to Maud. Veronica had to admit that she wasn't experienced, but she had considered their liaison more than satisfactory, but perhaps not so for him. Had he found her so immature that he had needed to race off to Orlando without any explanation?

*   *   *

The drive back to Rochester was pleasant as the intense heat of the day was decreasing, so they stopped at a roadside restaurant to enjoy a meal before going home. The remainder of Veronica's stay was similarly spent, though very carefully planned by Andy and Margaret, who alternated long trips, such as the ones to Letchworth State Park and Watkins Glen, with visits closer home. Rochester itself was a town very much like a British one, and she enjoyed a day there with Margaret. They window-gazed as they walked along happily together, and shopped in the shopping mall where Veronica admired the clock of all nations, waiting until the hour struck to watch the doors opening as it revolved, to reveal figures dressed in national costume of countries all around the world. At midday they went up in an outside lift to the top of a very high building where they had lunch in the Changing Scene revolving restaurant, which afforded a magnificent view of the city and surrounding area. Veronica was delighted to find that any previous inhibitions and doubts on either side had completely vanished, and after two glasses of rosé wine she and Margaret were like two giggling schoolgirls. In a way she felt she was helping Margaret to relax more. It couldn't be easy for her having two men to look after, and she didn't seem to have any girl friends to share some time with. Veronica knew that when the day came for her departure back to Groton Margaret was genuinely sad, as was Burt, but the goodbyes had to be said.

'You will come again now, do you hear me?' Burt insisted.

'You've been so kind,' Veronica said with a break in her voice. 'I don't like to impose, but if you'll have me just try keeping me away!'

The flight was called then and she went through the gate to the tarmac and with a last wave made her way to the aircraft. She had an hour now to sit and think affectionately of her newly found family—Grandfather, Margaret and Andy. Even he had become quite emotional when he'd said goodbye the previous evening. She didn't blame him for having the suspicions he'd not even tried to hide. Wouldn't she feel the same way in the circumstances? If someone had come looking for her father she knew how jealous she'd be capable of feeling, never mind the reason for their quest. It was a pity that everything came down to money in the end, but the twentieth century had bred a mercenary type of person, she thought.

Before reaching Kennedy Aiport Veronica looked at her tickets and discovered that she would have quite a wait before her flight back to Groton. She didn't mind, because there was always something to watch where hundreds of people were milling around. She decided to go to the Pilgrim Airline's desk and check in straight away in order to get rid of her suitcase, and while standing in the queue she noticed that there was an earlier flight to Groton, so when she reached the clerk she asked if there was any room on it. The girl shook her head and said there wasn't, so Veronica left her suitcase and turned round—to collide right into Oliver's arms!

She tried to speak, but he gathered her close against his chest and kissed her forcibly on her lips. Her head swam; what was he doing here? And why was he kissing her as if he had missed her when he had been with his beloved Maud? When at last he released her she asked heatedly: 'What on earth are you doing here? And if you don't mind, I don't like making an exhibition of myself!'

'I thought *I* was making an exhibition of you, darling. I also decided I'd better be here in case you got in bother.'

'I'm quite capable of travelling on my own without your help,' she said indignantly. She felt embarrassed, hot and unsure of herself, which was why she was being tetchy. Goodness knows, she thought, hadn't it made her day, having Oliver meet her here? By accident or design, though? That would make all the difference.

'You were glad of my help on a previous occasion, as I recall,' he said, lifting his eyebrows seductively. Damn the man! Veronica thought crossly. Why could he turn everything to his own advantage, and why did her heart turn a somersault at the very sight of him? He looked gorgeous. There was no other word for it—bronzed, a trifle leaner perhaps, his hair a shade lighter, and his eyes—well, he could kill with the blue of them, which could be steely blue with anger or as easily sky-blue with warmth, and she wished, really wished she could hate him. But love would not be eradicated, no matter how hard she tried, so she compromised by tossing her head defiantly, her own eyes a sharper green. 'I admit I was glad of your help that day, but I daresay I'd have managed. I did get to Groton eventually under my own steam.'

'You flew the plane?' he taunted mischievously.

Veronica pursed her lips, trying not to laugh. 'You know very well what I mean,' she said impatiently. 'You were going in the other direction.'

'That's right, when if communication had been more efficient we could have crossed the Atlantic together.'

'What are you doing here anyway?' she repeated.

'Returning to Brookville, the same as you, so I thought it was a good idea to catch you here at Kennedy.'

'But you didn't know what my travel arrangements were!'

'No?' He arched his eyebrows again, this time so wickedly that she felt as if her heart had jumped right down at her feet. 'My dear Veronica, in my position I have to make it my business to know where my staff are at all times, and what they're up to.'

She found her brain racing ahead of her and she wanted to retort: 'But your staff couldn't possibly know the half of what you get up to in jacuzzis and saunas . . .' but instead she said simply: 'So you got all the information out of Dave?'

'I do keep in touch with my staff when I go away on business.'

Veronica felt her cheeks flush darkly. Who was he kidding? Business—huh! Some business—funny business with Maud Kishnev, more like. Oliver placed his arm beneath her elbow. 'I don't know why we're standing here like lemons,' he said. 'Come along, there's a good restaurant and we've got time to eat before our flight. I want to hear all about your week's holiday in Rochester. You look well, Veronica, so I take it that it was worth while?'

'I've had a wonderful time, and my grandfather had no doubts about my origins because I'm so much like my grandmother. He knew all about my mother too, which made things so much easier. It was only Margaret's husband, Andy, who was a bit anti at first—and I can understand why. He thought I might be after any money there was going. Oh, there's so much to tell you . . .'

What was she thinking of? As if he was interested in her background! Maybe all he was after was a repeat performance of that lovely afternoon they had spent together, and the awful thing was that she knew she would give herself up to him again if the opportunity arose. It mustn't! She must see that she wasn't available for such assignations in future, and she'd need Dave to help her, she decided.

'We've got just over an hour and a half to wait for our flight,' Oliver said softly. 'I can think of more pleasant ways of spending that amount of time, but being stuck here at Kennedy restricts us.'

Veronica rounded on him savagely. 'Look, Oliver,' she said, so adamantly that she surprised herself, 'I'm tired of your persistent innuendoes. All right, you were kind enough to give me a nice day out, and what followed was a ghastly mistake which wouldn't, couldn't have happened if you hadn't planned it all beforehand, taking me to your bungalow for the only reason a man ever seems to have in his head.'

He looked momentarily stunned by her outburst, then his expression darkened with anger. 'How dare you!' he ground out between sharp, even white teeth. 'I thought what we shared that afternoon was something very sacred to both of us.'

'Sacred!' echoed Veronica. 'You wouldn't know the meaning of the word! And you really didn't have to meet me here, I am over twenty-one!'

'Then for God's sake behave as if you are!' he

snapped. 'I thought you didn't like making an exhibition of yourself—well, you're making an excellent job of it at this minute. Come along and we'll go to the restaurant —and . . .' he warned with brooding contempt as he took her arm roughly, 'don't think of creating any more of a scene here, or I'll pick you up and sling you over my shoulder!'

She knew he would too, so with burning cheeks she found herself being hustled along.

'I need to go to the rest room,' she said meekly after a few steps had taken them farther into the waiting lounge. She heard him sigh impatiently.

'Over there.' He pointed to the sign in the distance. 'And don't be all day.'

Veronica spent a quiet five minutes composing herself, then after applying a shade more lipstick she casually returned to Oliver, who was studying the menu outside the nearby restaurant. She didn't dare look up into his questioning eyes but allowed herself to be escorted inside to a window table. At least here she could concentrate on what was going on outside rather than on the man sitting opposite her. A jug of iced water was brought immediately with the menus, and she gratefully hid behind it until Oliver tapped the outside with his pen. 'Is the delectable Miss Summers at home?' Veronica lowered the menu and met his gaze. 'What can I tempt you to?' he asked, then with a click of his fingers and a self-rebuking pursing of his lips he rephrased his question. 'Sorry, what would you care to order?'

'I'm not very hungry,' she said. 'So I think I'll have soup and a beef sandwich.'

'That sounds fine,' and when the waitress returned he ordered the same for both of them. 'Now, Veronica, I think we'd better start again,' he said slowly. 'Tell me about your week in Rochester.' She looked up at him with aggression still in her expression. 'No, I really want to know,' he assured her quickly.

She didn't find it that easy to begin talking as if nothing had happened. She had made things bad between them. Of course that afternoon hadn't been a mistake, she had loved every minute of it, but now Oliver must believe that to her it had been as meaningless as it had been to him. She had the grace to look abashed and sipped the ice-cold water gratefully, then she told him how her grandfather lived with Margaret and Andy in a tree-lined avenue not too far from the airport.

'Niagara Falls was the highlight of the week,' she said, 'but I thoroughly enjoyed everything we did. Watkins Glen is a lovely beauty spot, and Letchworth State Park is huge, apparently known as the Grand Canyon of the east.'

'And do you plan to visit them again?' asked Oliver.

'I must—I mean, the year will soon pass, so for my mother's sake I must make the most of my time here.'

'Then remember that you'll have the winter months to consider. I don't advise a journey in that direction at Christmas, for instance.'

'We didn't get around to making definite plans, but we shall be keeping in touch.'

'Of course,' Oliver said idly, but Veronica read more into it than that. He didn't like the idea of her going off again. Maybe for some stupid reason he was jealous of her having succeeded in her mission which, she recalled, he had warned her against in the beginning.

She enjoyed the soup, sandwich, and coffee while Oliver quizzed her at length about all that she had done, and then she remembered to ask him if he had enjoyed his holiday.

'Not really a holiday, Veronica. Maud had a very difficult case. As you know, her field is brain surgery, she knows I'm interested in new techniques, so she asked me to go down and assist her, which I was pleased to do, though disappointed that it was necessary to have to end our day so abruptly. If that's why you thought it was a casual affair on my part, I'm deeply sorry.'

'I think it would be much better if we didn't mention it again,' said Veronica, hating herself now for her silly notions. She was the jealous one, not Oliver, and now she had spoilt everything. She persuaded him to explain more about Maud's case, and the time passed quickly.

Then their flight was called and soon they were aboard the small aircraft. She didn't think she would ever get used to flying this close to the cockpit, where she could see everything the pilot and co-pilot were doing, and she said as much to Oliver.

'You will,' he assured her. 'It's one of the safest aircraft in the sky, you'll learn to love it by the time you've been around a bit.' Once they were airborne he reached across to hold her hand, but there was no feeling there, he was just being protective. When they touched down at Groton, Dave was there to meet them. He looked quizzically at Veronica but could read nothing in her expression. She sat in a back seat corner of the car while Oliver, sitting beside Dave, soon embarked on an inquisition as to all that had happened at Brookville in his absence. Oliver said a curt goodbye to her when Dave dropped him off at the hospital and Dave carried on to Riverside.

'You off duty now, then?' Veronica asked, as she got out of the car and stretched.

'Yes. Bob Olsen's going to give Oliver a run-down of all our patients, and believe me, he won't go to bed until he's read up all their notes. He'll probably visit some of them too. He may give the impression that he can hand over to someone else, but he hates doing it, and when he gets back he's full of regrets.'

'Has he ever had cause for that?'

Dave laughed. 'No, but he can't quite convince himself that anyone else is capable of dealing with an emergency. I guess I'd feel much the same in his position. He's a great guy. He doesn't just go away and learn about new techniques, he comes back and shares it all with us. There'll be a special meeting of all interested parties very shortly, so that what he's been doing with Maud is fresh in his mind.'

Veronica felt the old suspicion creep back. Whatever Oliver had been doing with Maud Kishnev, whether at work or at leisure, would most certainly be fresh in his mind, she vowed. She told herself she wasn't being quite fair. He had admitted that he had known Maud for a very long time, but that didn't alter the fact that there could be more in it than being colleagues.

Brookville didn't seem strange to Veronica when she went back on duty the following day. She loved it, and was soon back in the swing of work, eager to tell Natalie, Gloria and Dave all about her week away during coffee breaks and in the evenings.

'I've got some news for you,' Dave told her one morning when they were doing a clinic together. 'Mrs Walcott said I was to tell you especially.'

'Oh, what?'

'She's decided to stay where she is. She's settled down with Mrs Curtiss very well and she realises how good it is not to have any worries, so she's going to sell up her home.'

'That's a bit drastic, isn't it?'

'It may never come to that, Veronica. We've persuaded her to stay where she can be cared for, and at ninety-three it can't be for much longer, so what does it matter? A neighbour has agreed to look after the house for the present. Mrs Walcott thinks that when she's well enough she'll be able to go back there occasionally to turn out her belongings, but I doubt that she ever will.'

'Oh dear, that's so sad!' sighed Veronica.

'How would you like to go and see her when we can get some time off together?' asked Dave.

'Yes, though that can't be for a bit, as I'm only just back.'

The suggestion was shelved for nearly two weeks. Veronica's car went wrong and needed some work doing on it, so she was dependent on other people for lifts in to work, though she noticed that Oliver didn't offer. They worked in harmony together because it was demanded of them, but he appeared to have detached himself from her socially. It broke her heart every time she worked with him, she loved him more desperately each day but his thoughts were obviously elsewhere. Jealousy was indeed a cruel emotion.

Some few days later during the midday break and

before Oliver had arrived to begin his clinic, Gloria came down to the Outpatients Department. 'I don't know whether you know,' she said, 'but it's Oliver's birthday today, so we've arranged a little surprise for him. Although you've got a Mrs Brown down for two o'clock that's a phoney patient, so if he gets too keen you'll have to stall him and say she hasn't arrived or you can't find her notes.'

'That won't please him,' said Veronica dubiously. 'What sort of a surprise? Is all the secrecy really necessary?'

'Wait and see. I'm trying to get everyone who can to join in the fun, so be prepared for a bit of a chaotic five minutes,' warned Gloria.

'Is it a cake or a present of some sort?'

'Very definitely a present, though we do have a cake in the cafeteria as well.'

'I wouldn't have thought Oliver was the type to like surprises being sprung on him. I hope you're not going to disrupt the afternoon session, don't forget he's got patients to see.' Veronica didn't much like the way Gloria glinted at her before dashing off again, but she supposed it was all quite harmless, though she found it difficult to tell lies when Oliver arrived and seemed to be in a hurry to begin seeing his patients. Veronica looked sheepishly at the clock on the wall.

'Yes, I know it's only five to two, Veronica, and it won't be time to go home for quite a while, so where's Mrs Brown?'

'She hasn't arrived yet.'

'Then give me her notes so I can familiarise myself with the reason I'm to see her.'

'I . . . I'm sorry, I don't seem to have them,' she apologised, fiddling with the pile in her hands. She was regretting being in on any surprise when suddenly everyone started arriving behind Gloria, who went first to wish Oliver a happy birthday, then some music came from somewhere, and through the assembled staff came a young girl wearing a velvet cloak. One glance at Oliver's face made Veronica wish she hadn't been caught quite so close to his desk. The Kissogram girl removed her cloak to reveal the briefest of bikinis, and with a feminine display of sensuality she went to sit on Oliver's knee, then read him a suitable greeting from the card she had brought, which was supposedly from the staff at Brookville. Veronica felt extremely sorry for him. He looked ill at ease, but he managed to smile and as everyone clapped and cheered he gave the girl a kiss before almost tipping her off his lap. Veronica could hardly bear to look at his growing angry expression, and she was glad when someone helped the girl into her cloak and hastily led her away. With horror Veronica realised that Oliver was staring directly at her.

'Thank *you* for that,' he growled. 'I'm afraid I'm not keen on practical jokes during working hours, Veronica. May I suggest we all get on with our work. We aim to give a service to sick people, so let's get on with it.'

'B—but . . .' Veronica stammered.

'First patient, please,' Oliver demanded, and when Veronica turned to go to the waiting area she discovered that the rest of the staff had deserted her. She supposed the joke had been aimed as much towards her as Oliver, and she too felt uncomfortable about the whole incident.

There was a strained silence between them. She wanted to tell him that it had been as much of a surprise to her as to him, but somehow she felt he was in no mood to accept such an explanation and probably wouldn't believe her anyway. When the last patient had gone from the examination room she plucked up enough courage to go to Oliver.

'Oliver, I had nothing to do with that little fiasco,' she said. 'I didn't even know it was your birthday.'

He was busy writing and barely glanced up. 'Don't make matters worse, Veronica. They always make me a cake in the cafeteria, so you could hardly not know. Just remember in future that I object to havng some dolly bird thrust upon me in public. I prefer to choose my own female company. I'm a traditionalist, a simple card would have been sufficient.'

Veronica sighed with no attempt to hide her aggravation.

'I had nothing to do with it, and I repeat, I did not know it was your birthday. I'm sorry if it's been ruined for you, but many happy returns anyway.' She turned and went back to her duties of tidying the examination rooms and placing clean gowns and sheets out in preparation for the following day. When she went to report off duty Oliver had already left. Often he worked on at his desk, so she guessed he had taken himself off to his apartment or gone up to the wards, anywhere as long as he didn't have to come into contact with her, she supposed.

She tried to think who could have arranged such a prank. Probably several of the staff had been involved, but one person must have thought up the idea initially. And why did Oliver imagine that she would do such a thing? She felt hurt at his assumption and determined to find out who it was. Gloria had definitely been in on it, so she'd have a word with her tomorrow, but later that evening someone knocked at her door quite late. She wasn't in bed, she wasn't even ready as she had been doing some odd jobs. She felt a little dishevelled and wasn't really up to receiving company at past eleven o'clock. She hoped it might be Oliver. She didn't care what she looked like as long as he had come to apologise for his accusation, which she hoped had now been disproved, but the masculine voice was not Oliver's.

'It's only me, Veronica,' Dave called.

She slid back the chain and opened the door. 'You're a late caller,' she said.

'I had to come. You must be feeling cheated, and it was rotten of Oliver to blame you when he had no reason.'

'I can't imagine why he should think I would do such a thing. I wouldn't know where to go to order a Kissogram, and I didn't even know it was his birthday, but I do appreciate that he'd be mad. In Outpatients of all places! Who could possibly be so stupid?' Veronica put the kettle on, knowing that Dave would like some refreshment. 'One of the interns, do you suppose?'

Dave stalked up and down the kitchen, and it was the first time Veronica had ever seen him really aggressive. 'I could kill that woman!' he gritted.

Veronica stopped in her tracks. 'Maud? Do you mean Maud?'

'Heavens, no! Gloria, of course. I wouldn't have thought even she could be so mixed-up crazy, but she obviously did it to put you in a bad light with Oliver. I can't be certain, of course, but when I'd recovered from seeing that girl come in and sit on Oliver's lap I noticed Gloria sneaking out of the door. I didn't think anything of it at the time, except that perhaps she felt embarrassed for Oliver, everyone knows she's always had a crush on him, but I didn't think she'd stoop as low as this.'

The kettle whistled and Veronica poured the water thoughtfully on to the tea-bags. She didn't want to add fuel to the fire, but it was Gloria who had set everything up with her, and she said so to Dave.

'Now I come to think of it, she made sure it was me who was with Oliver when the girl arrived,' Veronica went on. 'Mrs Brown indeed—I wonder Oliver didn't smell a rat then!'

'I think I'll give him a ring,' said Dave. 'He doesn't go to bed early and I don't think it's right that you should get the blame. But why? Gloria surely realises she'll get found out—but not until she's split you and Oliver up.'

'She didn't need to go to those lengths, there's nothing between Oliver and me anyway. I thought everyone knew about him and Maud?'

'They do, but it's fairly obvious that he's taken a shine to you too. Maybe he's said something to Gloria which makes her think there's more to your relationship than there is.'

Veronica felt awkward. There had been one day of intimacy. Surely Oliver wouldn't reveal any secrets to Gloria of all people, and she could hardly tell Dave what had occurred at his bungalow. He smiled as he gazed down at her.

'I guess we all know that if there wasn't Maud, then . . .'

'Well, you can put an end to rumours of that sort, Dave,' Veronica retorted readily. 'There's absolutely nothing between us. Oliver was just being protective towards me when he thought I was going to get into hot water looking for my grandfather. Now that I have and everything is fine he doesn't have to worry any more.'

'I believe he rang you at Howard Johnson's,' Veronica nodded. 'He was very uptight about you having gone there without his knowledge, and he made certain his homecoming coincided with yours, so he could meet you at Kennedy.'

'Did Gloria know that, I wonder?' Veronica asked intuitively.

Dave placed his mug down on the working surface with a thud, and shook his finger at her. 'You might well have hit the nail on the head, my sweet. She's well known for spying, listening to other people's telephone conversations, and I believe she may have heard Natalie telling me Oliver was angry when she told him you'd left for Rochester. She's very jealous of you, that's for sure. Well, I shall tell Oliver at the first opportunity,' he declared.

'Please don't, Dave,' pleaded Veronica. 'It'll look as if I'm trying to stir up trouble, and frankly I don't care who organised the so-called joke, I know it wasn't me, so he can think what he likes.'

Dave looked at her curiously, then changed the subject abruptly and Veronica hoped the incident was forgotten.

'Tomorrow evening?' he queried. 'Are you off?'

'Yes, I finish at four—why?'

'Be ready for me at six and we'll visit Mrs Walcott.'

'That'll be nice. What shall we take her?'

'We'll stop off on the way and buy something.'

'What about Jenny Pearson?' Veronica asked. 'Any news?'

'She—um—er—keeps in touch with Mrs W., I think, so maybe we shall hear something tomorrow.

172 NEW ENGLAND NURSE

Remember to ask the old lady.' Dave gave Veronica a sisterly peck on her cheek and said good night.

Veronica was thankful to get to bed, she felt very tired, but her mind buzzed with the prank Gloria had set up. Yes, it was Gloria, it must have been, she decided. The more she considered the prospect the more she was certain that Dave was right. How that woman must hate me, she thought, and she couldn't fathom the reason. She'd never had enemies before, and to attack her over Oliver was quite ridiculous. But maybe Gloria was besotted with him, just as she was, so perhaps it wasn't so ludicrous after all! She'd made not one enemy, but two, for Oliver had evidently lost his respect for her now, and that made her feel desperately unhappy, but she wasn't going to pursue the matter. He didn't think enough of her to accept her word, so what was the point of wasting her love on him?

The next day she assisted Dave and Bob Olsen with clinics, and was glad when four o'clock came so that she could go off duty. She passed Gloria in a corridor, so she nodded politely and went on her way. Natalie was at her desk when Veronica reported off duty and she whispered discreetly: 'Bet you wish you could get your own back on that one, don't you?'

'What would be the point? If she's got it into her head that she has every reason to be jealous of me then nothing I say will alter things. I just hope for her sake that Oliver never finds out it was her.'

'She must think we're all stupid. I'm sure she doesn't realise we all know who it was. After talking to Dave this morning I telephoned the Kissogram people and they confirmed that it was a Miss Tucker who'd paid for it to be sent to Brookville, so she can't deny it, but Dave says you want it dropped.'

Veronica shrugged. 'It's no big deal. Oliver doesn't know me very well if he thinks I'd arrange something like that during working hours—and at a hospital of all places! It might have been fun at a private party, but if I were in love with a man I'd hardly arrange for him to have a pretty girl slobbering all over him, would I?'

'I guess not. Oliver will find out, I can assure you.'

'But not from you—please, Natalie!'

'Anything you say.' Natalie shrugged and gave Veronica the kind of look that told her Natalie evidently thought she was mad. She preferred the matter to be forgotten. If Gloria got her kicks that way then who was she to argue? And no real harm had been done, except that now Oliver had lost interest in her. If, she thought sardonically, he had ever had any genuine interest in her in the first place. Maybe he was one of those men who needed to make a conquest occasionally to boost their ego. She had been that all right, and she was the one who had got hurt. If she didn't love him so completely she would right now be setting out to retaliate, but revenge was not her style.

When she reached her upstairs flat at Riverside she had time for a rest and in fact dozed off for nearly an hour. By now things didn't seem nearly so bad, and she looked forward to being with Dave, and visiting Mrs Walcott, anxious to hear what news there was of Jenny. She showered and changed into a soft, light woollen two-piece. It was late August and the evenings were decidedly autumnal. It was difficult to believe that she had been in Groton since the spring, but she felt satisfied that she had fulfilled her task, and it was good to have the folks in Rochester to telephone sometimes. She didn't know how long she would be able to go on working with Oliver, though, loving him but with no chance of expressing her love. Maybe the Agency could transfer her to a hospital in Rochester. Now why hadn't she thought of that before? There was no hurry, though, she'd need to think things out before making any drastic moves, and she didn't mention the idea to Dave when he came off duty at six o'clock.

'I've prepared tea,' she exclaimed when he urged her to hurry up. 'You can't have eaten, you've only just finished work.'

'It's too early, Veronica. I had the usual afternoon break, so let's get going. We must stop off at the shops, remember.'

'I hadn't forgotten,' Veronica said. 'Some biscuits would be nice, and I know Mrs Walcott's very partial to chocolates. Oliver promised her some when she first came into Brookville, but I expect he's had too much else on his mind to think about Mrs Walcott.' They wandered through the large store looking for anything they thought the old lady might need, and decided on various delicacies to eat as well as some soap and cologne. Veronica did some shopping for herself while they were there, and then they were off again to the large house run by Mrs Curtiss.

Mrs Walcott greeted Veronica like a long-lost daughter. 'I gave up hoping you'd come again,' she croaked. 'That's not very gracious of me, I know. Now sit down and tell me all your news.'

'I came to hear yours,' Veronica insisted. 'Are you managing to get about? I must say you're looking very well, so the chocolates won't do you any harm,' she laughed.

'You shouldn't have gone to this trouble,' Mrs Walcott told her. 'It's you I wanted to see. Now I wonder why I can see some unhappiness in your eyes. Dave tells me you've found your grandfather—how was it in Rochester?'

'I popped over while you were away,' Dave intervened.

Veronica chatted to Mrs Walcott, who today was sitting in her own large room. Dave sat a bit, then wandered to the window as if he couldn't rest, but Veronica didn't pay any attention to his restlessness until there was a knock at the door. Dave hurried to open it, and to Veronica's surprise Jenny came in looking radiantly happy, her arm tucked through that of the man who accompanied her. She almost fell on Veronica.

'Oh, it's great to see you,' she said excitedly, and while Veronica was desperately trying to work out what was going on, Jenny added proudly: 'Veronica, this is my father!'

It was then that Veronica noticed that Jenny's companion was an older man, yet still quite a handsome one.

He was of medium height with a shock of dark hair streaked with grey, and intense eyes, somehow not quite blue, yet not a dull grey. They shook hands, and Veronica felt at once that all the vibes she'd had about Jenny's father had been correct. He was a most charming man.

'Hello there, Veronica,' he drawled in what Veronica thought must be a Southern accent. 'I've heard a great deal about my daughter's "special" nurse. If I ever have to go into Brookville I hope you'll still be around.'

'You'll have to hurry up, then, Mr Pearson, as I'm only here for another eight months,' she told him.

'That's quite long enough to get sick,' he said jovially, 'but I think I'll take my daughter's word for how good you are—bedside manner and all that.'

Veronica was almost stupefied, too shocked to think of all the questions which crowded into her brain, and Jenny laughed at her.

'Biggest surprise of your life, eh, Veronica?'

'It certainly is, but how did you two get together again?'

'It's thanks to Dave here,' Jenny explained, looking at Dave with a little more than the deserved admiration. 'He telephoned my solicitor—he won't tell even me what he said, but it doesn't matter. That call brought Dad here to see me, and—well, we've got each other, and a lot of years to make up for. Mrs Walcott here played a part too, she persuaded me not to be so stubborn. I was so scared, even with Dave to support me, but Mrs Walcott assured me that it was what should have happened years ago.'

'There never was anyone else, Veronica,' Mr Pearson said. 'I guess I was too darned soft with my wife. She doted on Jenny and I got left out in the cold, and there's nothing more soul-destroying for a man than to feel rejected—ain't that right, Dave?'

Dave inclined his head and smiled. 'Got it in one,' he replied knowingly. 'I've always been a one for the girls, but mostly I just like their company, but you may as well know, Veronica, that Jenny and I are—' he shrugged and looked embarrassed like a lovesick schoolboy, 'walking out, is Mrs Walcott's expression.'

'It sounds delightful, and I can only wish you all the best,' smiled Veronica.

'I do have a confession to make, though—so I'd better get it over with. I felt that someone had to put Oliver straight about yesterday. In spite of what you may think, Veronica, he didn't take too much convincing, and he'd never have forgiven you if he hadn't been told the truth, so we thought, to make up to him for Gloria's little game, we'd book a table at Vauxhalls in New London to celebrate Oliver's birthday properly this evening. We wanted Mrs Walcott to come too, but she thinks it might be too much excitement for one day.'

'I just hope I'm going to live long enough to see you two girls safely married off—and remember, marriage vows are made to last a lifetime,' the old lady warned.

Veronica felt tears beginning to smart behind her eyes. She was so happy for Dave and Jenny, a match that was perfect, she felt sure, but for herself, whatever Dave might have said to Oliver and however much he wanted to believe her innocence, some doubt must surely lurk, and things couldn't be the same as that one perfect day. Another knock at the door prevented her from dissolving into tears, and in walked Oliver with what seemed an armful of flowers. He went up to Mrs Walcott and placed one bunch in her arms. 'For you, my dear,' he said, 'for helping to play Cupid for my registrar, and here's the chocolates I promised you if you behaved yourself.' He kissed her warmly. 'And as for you, Jenny,' he continued, 'I know I said we shouldn't interfere in a patient's private life, but maybe this one situation was the exception, and since you're taking on two men in your life I think you'll need a medal, but will flowers do for the time being?' Even when he had handed Jenny a bunch of flowers and given her a kiss, Veronica noticed that he still held another bouquet of flowers in his arms, and with a look of apology he gave them to her.

'This can't possibly make up for my rudeness yesterday, Veronica, and I can't expect you to forgive me, but

I am sincerely sorry for what happened. This time I simply refuse to make excuses for Gloria, and I've told her one more silly prank like that and she's out. It wasn't either the time or the place for such nonsense, but I should have known you better than to accuse you of something so irresponsible.'

Veronica wasn't able to answer as she fought to keep the tears at bay. She didn't care about his apology, or the fact that he genuinely believed she hadn't been a party to what had happened, but there was an aloofness in his expression which she found hard to take. Whatever he had felt for her previously had vanished, while her heart was overflowing with affection for him.

Dave came to her rescue by looking at his watch. 'I don't want to break up this bleeding heart session, but Mrs Walcott has to go down for supper, and we must get over to New London,' he said, guiding Jenny to the door. Oliver stood back as they all said farewell to Mrs Walcott, promising to visit her again when they could, but it was Mr Pearson who escorted Veronica to the car park.

'Perhaps you'll allow me the honour of driving you, Veronica,' he said. 'It'll give the young lovers a little time to themselves, and I want to thank you for all you've done for my Jenny. I know from an interview with Dr Linley that her successful rehabilitation is largely due to your kindness.'

Veronica shrugged. 'Well,' she said, half-turning towards Oliver, but he was already in his own car with the door closed and the engine revving, 'it was a team effort, Mr Pearson. Jenny's a nice girl and it was sad to see her so defeatist. Dave and I made it our job to show her reasons for living.'

Mr Pearson helped her into the front seat of his large saloon car, then followed Dave and Jenny. Oliver was nowhere to be seen. During the drive into town, Veronica learned that Jenny's father had worked his way up to sales manager for a plastics company. He was obviously in a good position and had made it his business to maintain Jenny and her mother until Jenny herself

had started to earn her own living. It seemed that his
wife had allowed him to keep her but refused to meet
him even halfway in a reconciliation.

'I could have asked for access to see Jenny,' he said,
'but Annie wouldn't have agreed readily, so for the sake
of Jenny being caught between two opposing forces I
stayed away and committed myself to my work. The
solicitor was never happy about it, and I believe he told
Annie he didn't agree with me on that. Jenny should
have got to know her father so that when she grew up she
could have judged for herself.' Mr Pearson paused, and
Veronica knew how difficult it was for him to speak of
the past without some emotion. 'Jenny didn't know it
until recently,' he went on, 'but I did visit Annie on
occasion after she was taken ill, but she didn't want me
before, and she seemed to want me even less then.'

'It must have been very hard for you, Mr Pearson,'
Veronica sympathised.

'Please call me Roy,' he said, then laughed. 'I've even
managed to persuade Jenny to call me that rather than
Dad!'

'I'm so pleased for you both, and especially for Jenny
and Dave. I knew she found him attractive, but then
patients do have a tendency to fall in love with their
doctor. I know Dave has been a bit fickle and I wasn't
sure he was ready to settle down, but evidently while I
was away he and Jenny saw a lot of each other.'

'Dave said he didn't want anyone else to get involved
when he contacted me through Jenny's attorney. Your
boss wasn't too keen on the idea, and I can understand
why—that's not his job, but I'm glad Dave was willing to
take a chance. Jenny and I have decided to make a clean
break now,' Roy went on. 'We're putting the old house
up for sale, we're going to divide the money, which will
give her and Dave a good start, so for a while she'll be
living down in New Haven, until they get married, but
she can always stay with me at my apartment. It's quite a
good size and I shall love to have both her and Dave
there any time. Annie and I never split the house up
because we both wanted Jenny to have it, now she insists

that I have a half share, which she'll get, of course, when I pass on.'

'It sounds as if it's all working out for you splendidly,' said Veronica, as they drew up in a wide side road just off the main street in New London.

She wished Dave had told her they would be eating out, and she said as much when he and Jenny joined her on the pavement.

'I could have saved myself all the bother of making sandwiches you didn't want,' she protested, 'and I would have dressed differently.'

'But you look wonderful,' Dave said. 'When do you ever look anything else?'

'Dave!' she admonished. 'Spare my blushes, and remember your fiancée.'

Dave quickly put his arm round Jenny's waist. 'She understands, don't you, honey? And she also agrees with me that you look stunning. That soft mulled wine colour suits you.'

'I thought how elegant you looked when you arrived, Veronica,' Jenny said. 'And Dave is right. You always look so well groomed, and you have such excellent taste.'

Veronica was glad Oliver was there ahead of them and urging them into the large old Victorian-style house.

'Have you been here before?' Roy asked Veronica.

'No. I've heard of it, but I hadn't got around to coming here. I believe it's quite a special place?'

'Built in 1846,' Oliver informed no one in particular, though Veronica assumed it was for her benefit. 'The original character of the house has been retained, along with its exhibits of old paintings and valuable collection of china. It's quite unique as they're only open on a Thursday evening to the public. They specialise in private parties.'

They were shown to a table in a conservatory which ran the width of the house at the back overlooking the garden, and along one side. The first course, crab cocktail, was served at the table with a glass of wine, after which they went through to the main room where huge tables were laden with a large variety of home-made dishes for the main course. There were vegetable and potato salads, noodles, cheese flan, as well as a variety of cold cuts to choose from.

'Oh dear,' Veronica said when she looked down at her plate, 'I think I've been terribly greedy!'

Dave, who was standing next to her, laughed, and indicated his own full plate. '*And* we can come back for a second helping,' he said. 'Follow Jenny on through the end door and you'll see the extent of the dining area. They don't cater for that many, but it *is* exclusive.'

Veronica passed through some open glass doors to the side conservatory which continued round to where they were sitting. It was certainly unusual, but quite charming, with all the tables candlelit. She found herself sandwiched between Roy and Oliver, but Oliver was not over-talkative even though the party was to celebrate his birthday. Jenny presented him with a gift-wrapped package as they were finishing their dessert of ice-cream or date pudding. He looked slightly embarrassed, but was delighted to find that it contained a stylish gold-coloured pen inscribed with his initials.

'That's very kind of you, Jenny,' he said graciously. 'But I don't deserve this.'

'Yes, you do, for being so generous with your time when I was in Brookville, and for investigating my problems enough to cure me.'

'I think you went quite a long way to curing yourself, my dear, and it's Dave and Veronica who did more than I did.'

'But you gave me Veronica,' Jenny insisted with a warm smile. 'And I want you all to know how much I appreciate all that you did for me.'

Congratulations were given to Oliver again as a small birthday cake was brought by the proprietors of Vauxhalls, and the evening ended pleasantly with a walk in the garden before the drive home. Veronica wished she had bought Oliver a present, just some token to show him that she cared, but it was too late now, and then the men were deciding who was to take the girls home.

'I brought Veronica,' said Dave, 'so I ought to see her safely back to Riverside, but I also want to see Jenny home, so we'll take Veronica first.'

'Please,' Veronica protested, 'I can get a taxi. I don't want to put anyone out.'

Roy began to apologise for not going in the right direction, but Oliver was adamant.

'I'll take Veronica home, it's on my way to Brookville, and thank you all for a lovely evening.' He was being very polite, and quite formal, and even in the car he seemed to find it awkward to speak to her. He might have apologised, she thought, but he had allowed the incident to come between them. When they reached Riverside Veronica invited him in for coffee. 'Thanks, Veronica, but I have a heavy day in theatre tomorrow, so I won't, if you don't mind. Thanks again, good night—oh, and by the way, would you report to Natalie in the morning, she's moving you to Women's Medical for a few weeks,' and after a quick peck on her cheek he got back into his car and took off down the drive as if the contact with her had scorched him.

She wished the tears which had threatened earlier would now materalise, but she remained dry-eyed, and as she prepared for bed she felt annoyance taking the place of bitter disappointment. Maybe she didn't love him at all, she told herself fiercely. It had just been another case of infatuation, and she'd show him that she just didn't care any more either. It wasn't Natalie's idea to move her, she knew, but Oliver's, so that he wouldn't have to see her almost daily, and as she stared into the night sky through the window she decided it would be the perfect solution if the agency would transfer her to a hospital in the Rochester area.

First thing the next morning she got up earlier than usual and wrote a brief letter to the agency explaining that she had been successful in tracing her grandfather, and wondered if there was a chance of being moved nearer to Rochester. On her way to Brookville she posted it.

CHAPTER TEN

As soon as Veronica reached Brookville the next day she knew she had acted too hastily. She felt so cross with herself that she was unable to discuss the matter with anyone else, so the burden grew to mammoth proportions. The day passed quickly enough as she had a new set of patients to get to know as well as different staff, but she didn't allow the dissension within herself to affect her work. Natalie was helping out on the women's medical ward as the head nurse there was off sick with influenza, so Veronica soon adjusted to the change. She knew well enough that Oliver had suggested a move so that he didn't have to work directly with her, but no one else was aware of the real reason, as it was to be expected that she would work in as many different departments as possible during her stay at Brookville.

She managed to forget her own dilemma for a few hours, and grew to like the homely atmosphere of the ward, but each time she went to the cafeteria for a break she saw either Oliver or Dave in the distance. On one occasion she actually sat at the same table as Gloria, but only the lightest of conversation passed between them, as Veronica was too busy wondering why she had been foolish enough to ask to be transferred to another hospital miles away where she wouldn't even get the chance to see Oliver, even from a distance. She tried to convince herself that there were plenty more fish in the sea, but after that day of exclusive pleasure spent in his company she knew she would never love anyone else with such devotion, nor could she contemplate becoming involved with another man.

To try to salve her conscience, that evening she telephoned Margaret in Rochester and told her the news that she had asked for a transfer.

'That's great—yes, great.' But it was obvious that

Margaret was not impressed, and her former suspicion was aroused.

'I don't suppose for a minute that they'll let me,' Veronica added with a weak laugh. 'After all, I'm consigned to Brookville and they'll expect me to stay here for the year. I don't know what time off I'll have over Christmas,' she babbled on, 'but it would be nice to meet up with you then.'

'We usually go to Andy's family for Christmas,' Margaret said, 'down in Florida. Dad finds the sunshine does him good, but we'll see you again soon, we hope.'

They chatted on about various things such as the charity shop which Margaret was helping with now, and after a few words with her grandfather Veronica rang off. She felt utterly miserable, and the letter from Ellie which had been waiting for her at Riverside hadn't exactly cheered her up. Her sister was off on some expedition or other, in the Lake District with a group of friends, so her father would be on his own. Reading it through a second time, Veronica felt her cheek muscles tighten at the news that a neighbour was going to look after her father in Ellie's absence. Her brain raced ahead. She supposed this woman was out to catch her father in her net. At first the mere thought of him marrying again filled her with apprehension, then she calmed and realised that it would be the best thing for all concerned. She might be quite wrong, of course. Their neighbours were very caring and Mrs Drake might be genuine in simply wanting to look after him. She was quite a nice person and had been a friend of her mother's, Veronica remembered. Home seemed so far away, and she almost wished that her year was up, but then she'd never see Oliver again, and that thought sent her into a black mood once more.

For several days she jumped every time the telephone rang, and watched for the post with mixed feelings, but when nothing happened she took each day as it came and immersed herself in her job. The ward took in diabetics, and women with chest complaints, so there were always injections to be prepared, medicines to give and numerous other jobs. Three weeks passed, and the only person Veronica confided in was Mrs Walcott whom she visited each week when possible. The old lady listened compassionately to Veronica's story of wanting to be nearer her family, then she stared at her with unseeing eyes, or so Veronica thought.

'So—he doesn't want you, so you're running away?' she said dreamily. 'I thought you had a bit more spunk than that, my girl.'

Veronica looked away and fiddled with the strap of her bag. 'It isn't like that, Mrs Walcott,' she said quietly.

'When you've lived as long as I have, Veronica, you get wise, you know. Perhaps you think he'll come running after you if you go away? Or is there another woman in the way?'

'Yes, there is, although he insists there's nothing between them now.'

'You've got close enough to discuss it, then?'

'No—he chose to tell me about her once, when I first came here. He probably regretted being so open to a comparative stranger, but he was feeling sorry for me when I first heard the true story behind my grandmother's lost love. I . . . I thought he was beginning to feel something for me, but then he went down to Orlando where Maud lives and works, and he's never been the same since. I suspect he thought I might be an easy conquest, but I let it be known that I don't go in for casual affairs.'

'That's to your credit. But I can't help feeling that you're making a mistake in letting him go so easily. Gloria Tucker will think she's won, you know.'

'She can think what she likes,' shrugged Veronica. 'At least I'm positive I haven't lost him to her.'

'But she may well think she's got a clear field with you out of the way, and men are funny creatures, Veronica. They often let themselves be caught by the most unlikely of women.'

'It's done now, Mrs Walcott—and I must take the consequences, though I have some reservations that they'll ever consider a transfer. Maybe a second year's extension nearer Rochester when I'm through at Brookville.'

'You stay and fight, my dear,' the old lady advised. 'I can tell you this, you'll not find a more worthy man to fight over than Dr Linley.'

Aged and weary though she was, Mrs Walcott could always lift Veronica's spirits. She never lost her sparkle or her love of life, and Jenny Pearson could vouch for that. Veronica's burden seemed lighter for the next week or two, and when she still heard nothing, not even an acknowledgement, she had almost forgotten about it when just as she was going for her mid-morning break one day, the head nurse of the ward called her to say that Dr Linley wanted to see her in his office at once. Veronica's heart lifted, then plunged to the depths of despair. Oliver had found out. He was the one who was going to tell her that either she couldn't go to another hospital or she was on her way! And suddenly she felt it in her bones that they were going to transfer her. Well, she thought, as she went down in the lift alone, if it depended upon him he would be only too pleased to say goodbye.

When she reached his office she knocked boldly, she must pretend she felt confident, and at his request she entered, to find him standing at the window with his back to her.

'You wanted me, Dr Linley?' she said in as natural a voice as she could manage.

For several seconds he didn't move, then he swung round and waved a letter in her face.

'I don't believe this,' he said. 'I just cannot believe it!'

'If it's about what I think . . .'

'What you *know* it's about, Veronica. Don't come the innocent with me!' He drew his breath in sharply and his face was dark with anger. 'You might have had the decency to come and talk this over with me first. What do you suppose the agency will think about Brookville when they get a request like this?'

'But . . . they know it's because I'd like to see more of

my grandfather and his family.' God, how she wished Margaret had invited her there for Christmas, but she didn't lie easily. 'There's nothing wrong with Brookville,' she said, trying to placate him. 'And I haven't said anything detrimental about it.'

Oliver stared at her, fury rising in his face so that she thought he was going to explode.

'You accused me of wanting you for one reason only—so I left you alone to cool things between us. My God, Veronica, I thought I'd made it plain enough that I care about you too much to ever let you go!'

She felt her chin quiver. Now what kind of a fool did he think she was? She hadn't come here to be abused, to be made a fool of! He came round to her side of the desk, waving the letter at her again. 'I wish I could believe that this is genuine, Veronica, but it isn't, any more than that I want to go to the moon! You're not getting any transfer. You're going to stay here and be a thorn in my side—unless . . .'

'Unless what?' she asked hesitantly.

'You can convince me that you don't love me. Go on, Veronica, tell me you hate and despise me.'

She looked up at him, so close that she could feel his warm breath fanning her hair, and smell the faint tang of cologne from his body—a body that was so masculine, so virile—no, of course she couldn't tell that big a lie, that she hated and despised him—he must know how much she loved him, and as the unspoken words burst in her brain she felt the tears finally trickle down her cheeks. Then she was in his arms, sobbing against his manly chest, probably ruining his smart lounge suit jacket, she thought illogically, but at least he knew she was devastated.

At last he lifted her chin with one finger. 'Go on,' he taunted. 'Tell me?'

'I love you, Oliver,' she said falteringly. 'But what's the use? You thought I was capable of pulling a silly stunt like that on your birthday, so you can't possibly think much of me, and then there's Maud.' She raised her eyes to meet his gaze. Her wet lashes fluttered uncontrollably, and then his mouth came down on her eyes to kiss away her tears.

'You silly girl,' he whispered. 'Such torture, and such a waste of emotion, not to mention time! I did apologise for blaming you. I thought you of all people would have understood just how hateful that kind of joke is in public. I'm not a killjoy, though, and if they'd tied you up in gold paper with pink bows I'd have carried you straight up to my apartment—and that's where we ought to be now, discussing this silly notion of yours sensibly.'

'But I'm not a sensible person,' said Veronica, drying her eyes on a clean white handkerchief she pinched from his top pocket. 'I assumed you already knew that.'

This time he kissed her hungrily on her mouth, forcing her lips apart so that she knew the passion she was arousing by merely being in his arms. 'Come along, my darling, we'll have our break upstairs,' and he led her to the nearest lift. Once in his apartment he threw off his jacket, put the kettle on, pushed her down on the couch and sat beside her. 'Now let's get Maud out of the way once and for all—well,' he added, 'you must understand, she'll always be top of my list of friends. We work well together, and I admire her skills. We think alike too, and she told me the very first time that she met you that you were going to be my wife. So we can't disappoint Maud, now can we? You will marry me, won't you, Veronica—and because I love you, not because Maud thinks it's right.'

Veronica laughed. 'I want nothing more than to be your wife, Oliver. I've thought of little else since we met, but especially after that magic day when you took me to your bungalow.'

'Me too,' he said, 'though I have to admit that when Maud rang and said she needed me it got my adrenalin flowing and I really did think I'd explained more fully to you why I was going down to Orlando. There was another reason there was such urgency in seeing her, though. The man she loves was being held in Russia, not because he'd committed any crime, political or otherwise, but because of his scientific knowledge. It's taken six years for him to gain his freedom, so she wanted me to meet him, and now they're soon to be married, so I hope you haven't made any arrangements for Christmas. You'll be spending it with me in Orlando, where it'll be warm and balmy. I'll show you Disney World and the Cypress Gardens—if we can find the time, of course. They want us to be witnesses to their union, and then they'll fly off to the West Indies for their honeymoon, and we can use Maud's cottage. How does that sound?'

Veronica just melted in his embrace. He had everything planned. The kettle had switched itself off, so Oliver made the tea and went to the telephone, explaining to the nurse in charge of the medical ward that Veronica had just agreed to marry him, so she would not be returning to the ward.

Veronica gasped. 'Oliver, whatever do you think you're doing?' she shrieked. 'The whole hospital will know now!'

'Exactly,' he said. 'You haven't changed your mind, have you?'

'No,' she said, rushing to him and hugging him in a bear-like embrace. Then she saw the letter lying on the work surface. 'Oh, what was in that letter from the agency?' she asked. 'Just out of curiosity.'

'Mm . . . I don't know whether I ought to tell you or not,' he teased as he pulled it just out of her reach. She chased him and he pulled her down on the couch until wonder and speculation was forgotten . . .

Later Oliver allowed her to read the contents of the letter, and she discovered that the agency would have been happy to transfer her in the circumstances, but it was necessary to ask Oliver's permission and request her release from Brookville.

'No way,' he said, planting tiny kisses on her eyes, nose and lips. 'I ought to be very angry with you for writing to them,' he added.

'You were already angry with me, as I recall,' Veronica reminded him. 'I really thought you despised me, so I felt it best to go elsewhere, but only because I loved you so much I couldn't bear the pain of rejection. As soon as I'd posted the letter to the agency I wished I hadn't.'

She cuddled up against him, content at last. After they had found time to eat, and returned to some semblance of realism, Veronica telephoned her grandfather and Margaret, who were delighted with the news, but Margaret was bursting with good news of her own.

'I'm pregnant!' she announced delightedly, 'and it's all thanks to you, Veronica. Your coming made Dad so happy, and I did what you suggested and set about trying to do charity work instead of *trying* to get pregnant.'

When Veronica explained that she would be going to Orlando for Christmas they insisted on making plans to meet there as they were very anxious to meet Oliver.

'Mm . . . I don't know about that, darling,' Oliver said dubiously. 'We shan't have too much time to spare.' He winked at her wickedly as he rolled her beneath him on the couch. 'Christmas is for loving and giving, and I want to give you all my love in return for yours. My New England Nurse is going to become my New England wife, and like the Pilgrims who settled here before us we'll see that we create our own little English family right here.'

She sealed his proposal with a kiss, thinking that maybe it was just the right time for her father to be getting married again. Being in love, loving the most wonderful man on earth, could only transfer happiness to other people.